SAVAGE JUSTICE

Robert Hardin

iUniverse, Inc.
New York   Bloomington

Savage Justice

This is a work of fiction. All of the characters, names, incidents, organizations, and dialogue in this novel are either the products of the author's imagination or are used fictitiously.

iUniverse books may be ordered through booksellers or by contacting:

iUniverse
1663 Liberty Drive
Bloomington, IN 47403
www.iuniverse.com
1-800-Authors (1-800-288-4677)

Because of the dynamic nature of the Internet, any Web addresses or links contained in this book may have changed since publication and may no longer be valid. The views expressed in this work are solely those of the author and do not necessarily reflect the views of the publisher, and the publisher hereby disclaims any responsibility for them.

ISBN: 978-1-4502-7242-1 (pbk)
ISBN: 978-1-4502-7243-8 (ebk)

Printed in the United States of America

iUniverse rev. date: 11/11/2010

Dedicated to my maternal grandfather, Andrew Jackson Davis, a full-bloodied Cherokee Indian I wish I learned more from when I was growing up.

Thanks to Kathryn Hardin and John Burney for their editing, creative suggestions, and moral support.

Special thanks to Janice, Steve, and Matthew Hall for authenticating details about the Tohono O'odham reservation, and for their helpful feedback in general.

PREFACE

A major character in this novel is a member of the Tohono O'odham Indian Nation and a resident of the tribe's reservation near Tucson, Arizona. The reservation's southern boundary borders Mexico and the problem of that country's drug smugglers coming through the reservation to sell their wares in Tucson and Phoenix is a centerpiece of this book's plot.

The Tohono O'odham People date back to at least the 15th Century and their reservation lies on a portion of their original Sonoran Desert lands. Although they were initially conquered by Spanish conquistadors, they never embraced Catholicism and their armed rebellion in the 1750's caused the Spanish to retreat. As a result, much of the People's traditions remained intact for generations. Their more peaceful yet just as intransigent resistance to the invasion of American civilization has allowed them to still practice the ways of their ancestors, worship L'Itoli (Big Brother), their Creator, and speak their own language.

CHAPTER ONE

On a splendid Friday morning in July I rose early in the master stateroom of *Felicia's Gift*, the 57 foot Morris sloop I lived aboard in the West Sayville, Long Island marina, and drove my Aston Martin DB 9 Volante to Manhattan with the top down.

Three years earlier I retired from a lucrative practice as a criminal attorney specializing in murder trials, sold my firm to my partners, and accepted a position as the Executive Director of the Innocent Prisoners Project.

Our offices were on lower Fifth Avenue across from Union Square and my mission for the day was to clear my desk for a long absence.

My employment contract with the Project allowed me to keep my trial skills sharp by occasionally taking on cases I considered egregious examples of unjustified prosecutions, and I would soon leave for Arizona to defend Ned Johnson, a Tohono O'odham Indian tribal police officer charged with the torture-murder of a Mexican drug smuggler.

My administrative assistant buzzed me on the intercom to say Jarrett and Jim were ready for our conference call. "They're holding on line six."

"Thanks, Cheryl."

Jarrett succeeded me as the managing partner of my former firm and Jim ran his private detective agency out of the firm's offices in Santa Rosa, California. I always retained both men to assist me in trials.

"Good morning. Are you guys up for a summer in the desert trying the case I told you about?"

Jim said, "To be honest, baking in a hundred plus degree heat doesn't sound like much fun."

"Gird yourself," Jarrett said. "We'll be on a noble quest for truth and justice."

"And for the Yankee dollar," Jim added. "When can I start invoicing the Project for my time, David?"

"As soon as you do something to justify your expense, Gumshoe. I thought you mastered Billing 101 when you were in law school."

"I did but I found investigating more to my liking and since I can't charge anywhere near what you shysters do, billing is a sensitive subject with me."

"I'll authorize hazardous duty pay for you having to toil in overbearing weather conditions. Here's the plan. I'll fly my jet to Santa Rosa in the morning, pick you two up, and take us to Tucson. We'll interview our client over the weekend and get ready for the trial's first preliminary hearing on Monday so have fond farewells with your lovers tonight. We're off to fight a war with the United States government, one of our favorite adversaries."

Jarrett said, "I only recommended a few changes to the motions you emailed me, David. Impressive work."

"Thanks. Cheryl incorporated your changes and filed the motions with the federal judge and prosecutor in Tucson. I hope they now know we won't put up with business as usual."

"I'm sure they do. The motions are by no means routine."

Jim said, "How do you pronounce the Indian tribe our client belongs to?"

"TOW-HONE-OH AH-TOOM."

"Got it. What time are you landing at the Sonoma County Airport tomorrow?

"Around midday. Don't bring your Ace Detective School kit. And Jarrett, leave the alligator skin briefcase behind. I want us to look like we're serious and professional."

"Does this mean you won't be wearing your Mickey Mouse beanie in court?" Jim asked.

"Probably." As always, Jim's sense of humor left me with a grin.

My next conference call was with Ned's federal public defender and the Project's Tucson office manager to confirm the plan for them to have dinner with my associates and me on Saturday evening.

Charlie Nelson, our Tucson manager and Dean of the University of Arizona law school, said, "David, knowing how much you like an after-meal pipe, I made us seven p.m. reservations at McMahon's Steak House. They have a smoking bar and are only a short drive from your hotel."

"Perfect. Eating a pound of blood-red meat will give me the strength to wage combat in court on Monday."

Savage Justice

Drew Patterson, the federal public defender, said, "McMahon's a top of the line restaurant but their prices are too steep for my budget."

"The Project is paying the tab so you can eat and drink to your heart's content, Drew. Have you both filed your *amicus* briefs in support of my motion for a larger representation of Indians on the jury?"

Charlie said he was still refining his and would send the final version before the end of the day. Drew said he'd already transmitted his to the judge.

I thanked them both then reached Douglas Axelrod, the Assistant U.S. Attorney assigned to the case.

"Hello, Mr. Armstrong. I've received copies of your motions challenging the indictment, the make-up of the jury pool, and demanding immediate discovery. You're a renowned attorney so I expected you to come to town looking for a fight but I didn't anticipate you bringing an elephant gun. What got your dander up? You've deluged me with paperwork."

"The case against my client is so weak I'd be subject to accusations of ineffective assistance of counsel if I didn't make these pre-trial moves. The indictment is indisputably defective. And an original and well-reasoned challenge to the systematic exclusion of Indians from Arizona juries is long overdue. I'll rattle the timbers of the federal courthouse so loudly on Monday you'll think the area's having an earthquake."

"I'm working on correcting the indictment but I'll have to defend our jury selection process. As for your demand for me to make discovery at the hearing, I'll furnish you everything in my file."

"Has a decision been made on seeking the death penalty for Ned?"

"Not yet. I'm hoping I can announce our intention on Monday."

"I appreciate your cooperation and I look forward to meeting you in person, Mr. Axelrod."

Those calls out of the way, I met with Will, our assistant executive director, and felt confident leaving him in charge. We were well on our way to another record year of exonerating death-row prisoners through DNA testing.

Will said, "David, I've been meeting with the managers and staff of our offices in Illinois, Indiana, and Ohio for the past two weeks so all I have is bits and pieces of secondary information about your new case. I'd love to hear the whole story from you?"

"Then you shall. I'll give you a little background first. The Tohono O'odham Indian Reservation near Tucson, Arizona shares a seventy-five mile wide border with Mexico. A steel fence recently erected by the Border Patrol is preventing vehicles from entering the reservation from that perimeter so Mexican drug traffickers are bringing in marijuana on their backs and bribing or intimidating Indians to drive the goods to Tucson or Phoenix for them.

Indians who take advantage of the cash offers are learning the stiff penalties federal drug laws mandate, and the Indians who refuse the bribes are learning how brutal the smugglers can be.

"The horror our client, Ned Johnson, a lieutenant in the reservation's police department, witnessed is typical of what's happening to the Tohono O'odham people. The day his life changed forever he was off-duty and on the way to visit his family in a section of the vast reservation. He parked his pickup by an outbuilding to prevent stirring up dust and as he walked toward the front door of the adobe home he grew up in he heard screams. He grabbed his rifle from the pickup then stealthily worked his way around the property to a side window of the house. What he saw chilled him to the bone. His father and mother lay dead on the floor with their throats cut so deeply their heads were barely attached. His fifteen-year old sister was still alive and crying out but a Mexican man was holding a knife under her chin with one hand and molesting her breasts with another while a second Mexican man raped her. Ned fired his rifle at the man holding the knife. The shot missed, the knife-holder fled out a rear door, and the rapist opened fire on Ned with an automatic pistol. Ned fired back and wounded the rapist in the stomach but as the rapist fell he continued shooting and several bullets struck the young girl's chest. Ned burst inside to find her lifeless. Overcome with grief and anger, he tied the barely conscious Mexican's hands and feet, took him to a remote area of the desert, staked out his body in a spread-eagle position, and left him unprotected from the scalding mid-day sun and desert creatures. Ned is now charged with torture-murder and facing a possible death sentence."

"Is he remorseful?"

"Not in the least. When I decided to take Ned's case a few months ago I visited him in prison and asked if he had any regrets. 'Only one,' he said. 'I now wish I'd skinned the Mexican alive before I let the predators feast on him.'"

"How did the authorities find out Ned was responsible for the Mexican's death?"

"Ned drove his pickup to headquarters and turned himself in to his police chief."

Burt and Arthur, the Project's co-founders, invited me to have lunch with them at Katz's Delicatessen and Arthur took us to the Lower East Side establishment in his cavernous Chrysler 300 sedan.

Arthur and I ordered corned beef on rye sandwiches and Burt said, "The same for me but with lean meat only."

Our sassy waiter with an unadulterated Jewish accent left us after quipping, "Vich way you want the meat to lean?"

When he came back with the sandwiches he stood by with his arms crossed until Burt tasted his corned beef.

"You like?" he asked Burt.

"Yes. It's very good."

"It's not lean," the waiter deadpanned and left us again.

Burt chortled and Arthur, between bites of the succulent brisket, said, "David, how long have you been lobbying for the American Anesthesiologists Association to sanction doctors who participate in the lethal injection of prisoners?"

"At least two years."

"Making any progress?"

"Some."

"More than you might know. Although the official announcement won't be made until tomorrow morning, I have a friend on the AAA's board and he informed me that doctors who henceforth assist or consult in lethal injection executions will lose their certification effective immediately. The rule will be ironclad. Congratulations. Your long work paid off."

I beamed. "What fantastic news."

"Indeed," Burt said, raising his cream soda.

Arthur and I raised our sodas in kind and, at his station across the room, our waiter lifted a glass of water to us, no doubt thinking we liked the food so much we were toasting him.

Burt said, "We were thinking of throwing a party in the office after work to celebrate but you're probably preoccupied with the upcoming trial in Arizona and would like to leave early to be ahead of the commute."

"I would. Friday's are brutal on the Long Island Expressway."

Arthur said, "You're always at or near the top of every list of the best criminal attorneys in America and you've recently shown you're more worthy of the ranking than ever by winning a new trial for Charles Manson, of all people, then convincing a tough New York City judge to sentence a mercy killer to nothing more than probation. But how in Heaven do you expect to help an Indian reservation cop who gut shot a Mexican drug smuggler and tied him to stakes in the desert to be eaten alive by wild animals?"

"I'll employ a favorite strategy of the legendary Texas lawyer, Racehorse Haynes, and ask jurors to forgive Ned for ridding the world of a man who deserved to die. In trial after trial Racehorse proved jurors would let a killer go if they believed the victim needed killing."

Burt said, "An unvarnished argument for jury nullification a federal judge will surely curtail. And what about your procedural assault? Have you asked anyone other than us to file friend of court briefs in support of your claim that a trial in Pima County, Arizona would violate your client's Sixth Amendment right to a jury of his peers?"

"Yes. You're in distinguished company. Using my position as the current honorary President of the American Criminal Trial Lawyers Association, I also imposed on last year's President of ACTLA; the Director of the American Civil Liberties Union; the head of the Arizona Bar Association; the Chief Justice of the Arizona Supreme Court; the Chairwoman of the Native American Legal Rights Organization; our Tucson office manager and Dean of the University of Arizona law school; and a Tucson Federal Public Defender to buttress my claim."

"A blunderbuss approach," said Arthur.

"The prosecutor expressed a similar reaction but I don't see the point of subtlety in this case. Our client is in danger of being summarily processed and executed in a racially-biased Arizona system of justice. I will be heard."

"As you always are," Burt said. "We're glad to have you doing so on behalf of the Project."

On our return to the office Cheryl and I shared a goodbye hug and she said, "I'll miss you but I promise I won't contact you unless a three-alarm fire breaks out."

"You're so efficient I'm sure you could even deal with that. Remind me to give you a five dollar raise at your next salary review."

"Thanks, Boss. Your generosity is unbounded."

Back on my boat by six, I changed into casual clothes and went on deck to smoke a pipe and drink a scotch on the rocks.

I was feeling quite relaxed from the tobacco and whiskey when my cell phone rang and I heard the melodious voice of Felicia Bates-Baxter, California's senior U.S. Senator and the long-time love of my life. Felicia was a tall, shapely woman with gleaming black skin. The society columnist of the *Washington Post* rated her the most glamorous woman in D.C. until Michelle Obama came along. The columnist then said it was a toss-up between the two. I considered the First Lady a knockout but my vote was for Felicia.

I asked how her day on Capitol Hill had gone.

"Gone is the right word. When weekends approach the Senate is as empty as former President Bush's brain. Most members are more interested in getting out of town than working a five-day week to address the nation's enormous problems. Now that I've vented, I'll come down from my perch and ask if you're all set for your stint in Arizona."

"I'm packed and ready and looking forward to challenging the accusation of premeditated murder. Considering the provocation, I believe second-degree murder is the more appropriate charge."

"As you know, I sit on the Judiciary Committee and the case has generated considerable criticism of the Indian policeman's prosecution. With any luck you may be able to pull off another of your courtroom miracles."

"We'll see. Arizona jurors tend to be conservative. They recommend the death penalty more often than jurors in any State except Texas."

"You've reminded me why I rarely go to the God-forsaken place but I'll soon be nearby. Congress will recess for the month of August and I plan to spend the vacation in my San Francisco Bay Area house. Maybe you can come visit me a time or two?"

"Not until after the trial. When I visit I don't want to be thinking about anything but you."

"How nice. Have a good rest of your evening, my lily white lover."

"You too, my ebony black goddess."

I walked over to the wharf to have dinner at the Wheelhouse Restaurant and the owner, Yasky, said, "Hi, Mr. A. I saw a piece in the *New York Times* about your new case in Tucson, Arizona. I'm glad you're finally defending somebody besides a scumbag. The Indian sounds like an all right guy who did the right thing to the man who killed his family. I have a jury letting him off."

"From your lips to God's ears, Yasky."

I enjoyed a plate of fresh fish and a glass of wine then went back to my floating home for a full night's sleep.

CHAPTER TWO

Very early the next morning I ate a light breakfast on board, secured *Felicia's Gift*, and made the ten mile drive to McArthur Airport in the Aston Martin.

In preparation for my trip to Santa Rosa, California I made arrangements to land in Corcoran, California on the way. Corcoran was near the San Joaquin Valley prison where I met with Charles Manson to talk about his retrial. A budding young pilot named Billy Franklin hung out at the small airport and we became friends. I was looking forward to seeing him again and telling him about the surprise I had in store for him.

I opened my hangar to park the convertible in front of my vintage, indigo blue Jaguar XK-150 Cabriolet. The other possessions I kept in the hangar were a Beechcraft Premier jet and an ICON A5 single-engine amphibious aircraft. When I once defended my collection to Burt and Arthur by saying, 'the one who dies with the most toys wins,' Arthur's retort was, 'the one who dies with the most toys is still dead, Sucker.'

An employee of the company I rented the hanger from used a tractor to pull the jet out onto the tarmac. I then went aboard, spooled up the turbines, and contacted the FAA to activate my flight plan.

"Beech Jet November Nine Bravo Foxtrot Delta, you're cleared as filed direct to STS with stopovers in OKC and CRO. Following take-off, climb and maintain flight-level three-zero-zero and call departure control on frequency one-thirty three point three."

I repeated the instructions and the controller said, "Read back correct. Taxi to runway one-eight and call the tower when you're ready to leave."

"Roger," I replied.

I was in the air at seven a.m. When I reached the assigned altitude of thirty-thousand feet I adjusted power and trim to achieve the Premier's maximum cruising speed of five-hundred eighteen miles an hour, which left most airliners in the rear view mirror.

The cross-country trip to Corcoran, including a pit stop at Oklahoma City International for refueling and a cup of coffee, totaled five and a half hours but due to the left coast's earlier time zone it was only nine-thirty in the morning when I guided the swift Beech onto Corcoran airport's single runway.

Billy was standing near the fuel ramp and motioning me to a parking space. I was struck by how much taller he'd become in the few months since I last saw him but I shouldn't have been. Recently graduated from high school, Billy was at the age when most boys experience a spurt of growth.

"Hey, Mr. David," he said as I came down the plane's stairs. "Are we going for a spin around the block in the jet as usual?"

"Not today, Billy. I have something else in mind. Are you still taking flight lessons?"

"Yes, sir. I've already earned my private pilot's license and I'm working on my commercial."

Pointing to a Piper Aztec on the ramp, I said, "Where's the person who flew that twin here?"

"Inside the office having coffee. You want me to get him?"

"Please."

Billy scurried off and returned with a neatly dressed man in his thirties.

"David Armstrong?" he asked.

"Yes. Good to meet you, Kevin Burton. This is Billy Franklin, the young fellow you'll be training."

Turning to Billy, I continued. "Kevin is a flight instructor with King Aviation at the county airport in Hanford, Billy. I used some of the money from the educational fund I set up for you at the United California Bank downtown to prepay for Kevin to give you flight lessons in the Aztec until you receive multi-engine and instrument ratings. I have time to go on the first lesson with you today. Up in the air, Junior Birdmen."

Bouncing with excitement, Billy followed Kevin to the plane, watched him perform a pre-flight inspection then did as Kevin asked and sat in the cockpit's left front seat. I settled in the rear and Kevin positioned himself in the co-pilot chair next to Billy.

Kevin said, "Billy, before we get started I want to tell you about the Piper Aztec. You friend David specifically asked for an Aztec because the plane is perfect for your purposes. You probably would've preferred a sports car of the sky like a Beech Duke. What you've got is a flying station wagon—a forgiving, gentle, stable light twin that's the only one in its category capable of climbing on one engine fully loaded."

Following the short lecture Kevin showed Billy how to start the engines, after which Billy taxied the Aztec to the runway and took off with only a little help from Kevin.

Next Kevin talked Billy through a series of stalls and slow-speed turns before practicing touch and go landings first at Corcoran then at the tower-controlled Hanford airport.

During the flight I called Clara Robinson, the owner, publisher, editor, reporter, and photographer of the *Journal,* Corcoran's weekly newspaper to alert her to Billy's latest doings. She and I also become friends during the Manson retrial.

Kevin ended an hour of instruction by turning off the left engine and demonstrating the single-engine recovery procedure. When Billy was able to successfully repeat the procedure Kevin restarted the left engine and told him to make a final landing at Corcoran.

Mrs. Robinson was on the viewing platform above the airport office clicking away with her Nikon camera. Billy followed my cue and waved at her as he brought the Aztec to a stop nearby.

Before Kevin let us out and headed back to Hanford Billy made an appointment for another lesson the next day.

Mrs. Robinson came down from the roof to snap closer photos of us and say, "There. I've got enough for a big spread on our future airline pilot and winner of a twenty-five thousand dollar scholarship for having the highest grade point average in this year's graduating senior class. Thanks for the tip, David. It's good to see you again but I have to run. I'm covering the city council meeting."

She dashed to her car and Billy said, "Thanks, Mr. David. Flying the twin was a kick."

"You're welcome. I want you to have as many ratings as possible when you enroll at Embry-Riddle University so you can transition to their jet trainers more quickly. How did you settle on going there?"

"My high school counselor helped me make the choice. Both Ohio State and Purdue offer degrees in aviation and have their own air strips but airlines hire more pilots from Embry-Riddle than any other school in the country. We also figured their Daytona Beach, Florida location's favorable year round weather will allow more flying time."

"When do you start?"

"Next January. Four years later I'll have a Bachelor's Degree in aeronautical science and an air transport pilot ticket. I'll spend five years or so flying Boeings or Airbuses for a major carrier and by that time you may be too old to push the throttle of your jet any more and I'll be ready to pilot for you."

"Wipe that grin off your face, you little whippersnapper, and show your elder some respect. When I spoke with the UCB trustee he said he was ready to disburse tuition payments and living expenses for you whenever you need them."

"I spoke to him too the day I went to the bank to deposit the twenty-five thousand dollar scholarship check. He wouldn't put the money in the account you established so I opened one of my own."

"That was best. His fiduciary responsibility limits what he can and can't do. Congratulations on the award, Billy. I need to take off. I'm picking up a couple of associates in Sonoma County then flying us to Tucson, Arizona where I have a new trial starting. Stay in touch as you've been doing. I really like hearing what's going on with you."

I arrived at the Charles Schulz Sonoma County Airport in Santa Rosa at eleven-forty a.m. and found Jarrett and Jim waiting for me in the general aviation terminal.

Jim was wearing a chambray shirt, jeans, and cowboy boots, all obviously new and I said, "I see you're outfitted for Arizona."

"If he was going to a dude ranch, he would be," Jarrett said.

"You're just jealous because there were no black cowboys on the Old Chisholm Trail," Jim rejoined.

I said, "Actually there were lots of black wranglers but you have to dig deep into the history books to learn the little known fact."

We ate lunch in the Red Baron Café then made the hour and a half hop to Tucson.

The city was surrounded by mountains and as we descended over the Santa Rita Range to the west we saw hundreds of decommissioned bomber and fighter planes in the mothball fleet at Davis-Monthan Air Force Base.

A controller in Tucson International's tower cleared me to land and reported windy conditions with a temperature of a hundred and two degrees.

Thermals rising from the Sonoran Desert resulted in moderate turbulence and a bumpier arrival than I would've liked but neither we nor the plane suffered any damage.

I taxied to the Executive Terminal, arranged for the jet to be refueled and hangared, and picked up the Range Rover I'd reserved.

The heat was so intense we went from one air-conditioned oasis—the vehicle—to the next—the Radisson Suites.

After check-in we congregated in my quarters, which I found quite acceptable for the economical rate Cheryl negotiated. One room was furnished with a king-size bed, a large bathroom, and a separate dressing area. The sitting room featured a couch, chairs, flat-screen TV, kitchenette, small dining table, desk with internet connection, and a private balcony facing east.

I took advantage of the balcony to have a quick pipe smoke while Jarrett prepared the gin and tonics we all decided on even though we were a couple of hours ahead of our regular drinking time.

We settled in chairs around a coffee table and I said, "Tonight at seven we're having dinner in a steakhouse with Charlie Nelson, the UA law school Dean and manger of the Project's Tucson office, and with Drew Patterson, Ned's federal public defender. Tomorrow morning we have a ten o'clock appointment to talk with Ned in a federal prison on the outskirts of town."

"Have you visited him before?" Jim asked.

"When I decided to accept his case I came out and met with him. I also saw Charlie, Drew, Jesse Rivas, the chief of the tribal police department, and Emily Crenshaw, Ned's girlfriend. Chief Rivas gave me a map of the Tohono O'odham reservation on which he'd marked the location of Ned's trailer and his family's house. Both are isolated from Pisinimo, the nearest small settlement. Still, the Mexicans' brutal assault on Ned's family was a brazen move."

"I did some online research and learned attacks on the O'odhams by Mexican smugglers are commonplace. One of the articles I read quoted a Border Patrol Agent as saying the smugglers are mean and desperate and will cut the throats if anyone who crosses them."

"Part of your investigation in this case will be documenting these attacks. The more you find, the more I can mitigate Ned's behavior."

I took the map out of a file folder and handed it to Jim. "You can have this. The reason I rented a Land Rover instead of a conventional car was to give you the means to get around on the reservation. Rivas says only State Routes 86 and 232 are paved. The rest of the roads are dusty, deep-rutted, dirt trails accessible only by four-wheel drive vehicles. Did you bring your registered handgun?"

"No. It's too much hassle even when I'm traveling in a private plane."

"You should be armed when you're on the reservation. The smugglers spot the Range Rover and you'll be ripe for a carjacking."

"I'll buy a rifle and shells and store them behind the front seats. What else do you need me to find out?

"Let your well-trained nose lead you. Start by talking to Chief Rivas. He's a frank and intelligent man and very sympathetic to Ned's plight. Ned's girlfriend, Emily Crenshaw, is someone else you should meet. She comes from a wealthy family in Marin County, California but she's lived on the reservation for years and is the financer and co-founder of the Tohono O'odham Nation

Community Action, a non-profit organization that's helping the Nation's members give up their high-fat, high-sugar diet and cultivate and eat the foods of their ancestors. Also see what you can find on Fabian Ruiz, the bad guy Ned killed. His ID indicated he lived in Sonora, Mexico. And I'll want you to check out all the prosecution's witnesses. We'll find out who they are in Monday's preliminary hearing."

Jarrett refreshed our drinks and said, "David, I've boned up on the Federal Code of Criminal Procedure and there are no recent changes of any import. Is the government still considering seeking the death penalty?"

"I assume so. I spoke with the lead prosecutor yesterday and he said he may announce their intentions in the hearing."

"Was he in receipt of your motions when you talked to him?"

"For sure and he sounded bowled over by them."

"I can imagine. The challenge to the make-up of the jury is a long shot but I think you found a fatal flaw in the indictment that will force the judge to reduce the charge against Johnson from first to second-degree murder."

At a quarter to seven we went downstairs and used the Land Rover's GPS to guide us to McMahon's Steak House.

Charlie Wilson and Drew Patterson were waiting for us at a table on an outside patio. The heat had dropped considerably in the wake of the sunset and we were comfortable in the night air.

After a waiter brought menus and took our drink requests Drew handed me a manila folder. "Here are copies of everything in Ned's file for you, David. I sent Judge Warren's clerk a notice of withdrawal from the case so you're now officially Ned's attorney."

"Thanks, Drew. Tell us about Judge Warren."

"Like most federal judges he won't risk political fallout to protect a defendant's rights unless you cite him so much black letter law and binding precedent he's forced to do the right thing. The blitzkrieg of motions from you and your supporters was the talk of the Tucson legal community today. Warren is apparently stunned and there's widespread dissension in the ranks at the U.S. Attorney's offices. Charlie has the inside knowledge on all this."

The waiter arrived with martinis for all of us and Charlie said, "Let's choose our food first. Anything you order here will be good but I highly recommend the center-cut New York strip steaks."

We unanimously accepted Charlie's recommendation and I selected two bottles of robust Argentine reds for the table then said, "All right, Professor. Tell us what you know or we'll beat it out of you?"

Smiling at my impatience, he said, "Some of my law students are part-time interns in the U.S. Attorney' office in Tucson so my pipeline gushes.

Kaya Kabotie, who's in charge there, is a Hopi Indian and she agrees with your take on the jury pool. She's also opposed to capital punishment for Ned Johnson and has threatened to resign if Thomas Sloan, the U.S. Attorney, decides to seek the death penalty."

"Which poses quite a problem for Sloan," added Drew. "He promoted Kaya to her position with great fanfare and self-touted praise for his policies on gender and race. But he considers a Johnson a vigilante and wants to make an example of him."

I asked where Douglas Axelrod, Ned's prosecutor, stood in the debate and Charlie said, "Squarely behind Kaya. She inspires great loyalty from her associates. Sloan, on the other hand, is a prig who's universally disliked by persons inside and outside his department. A while back Janice Ott, the Presiding Judge of the Ninth Circuit Court of Appeals lampooned Sloan for his legal ignorance when she reversed a conviction he obtained as an Assistant U.S. Attorney. In her still widely circulated opinion she said he must've received an equal opportunity appointment for men with pompadour hairdos since she could discern no real qualifications for the job. Sloan is doubly embarrassed now because he personally came to Tucson to ask the grand jury to indict Johnson for torture-murder without bothering to check the Code. As you discovered, torture is not an element of federal first-degree murder. Nor is torture a federal crime so all Sloan can use his indictment for is toilet paper."

Our dinners were so filling we disdained desserts and went to the smoking bar for coffee and snifters of Taylor Flagate twenty-year old tawny port.

Charlie, Drew, Jarrett, and Jim chose H. Upmann cigars from the choices they were offered and I lighted a pipeful of a Balkan Sobranie blend I brought with me.

We savored the taste and aroma of our tobaccos and the vintage port and Drew said, "David, I was impressed—flabbergasted is more like it—by your zealous defense of Charles Manson in his retrial. As a public defender I can't choose who I represent and I'm assigned some pretty unsavory characters. You have a choice yet you seem to go out of your way to find odious clients. I wouldn't be surprised to hear you're defending Osama bin Laden next."

Jim moaned. "You asked for this, Drew. Your question gives David a chance to get up on his soapbox again."

I waved Jim off as if he were a pesky fly and said, "I'll give him the short version of the speech, Jim. Criminal attorneys have no right to pronounce moral judgment on persons accused of crimes, especially those accused of the most loathsome ones. Those defendants need effectiveness of counsel more than anyone. If we criminal attorneys don't provide that constitutionally guaranteed right, who will? As for my personal feelings, I have a natural aversion to prosecutors and a strong sense of fair play so saving unarmed clients from being sacrificed to Government trained gladiators provides me great satisfaction."

"Did freeing one of the most demonic mass-murderers in history satisfy you?"

"It satisfied my desire for justice."

"Justice? Did you really believe Manson was innocent?"

"Innocence is not a word I would ever apply to Charles Milles Manson, Jr. I'm positive he wasn't legally guilty of any of the murders, though."

"A fair answer. Part of me really wanted to know and another part of me was playing the Devil's advocate in hopes a fire would ignite in my belly like it did when I first began my career as a public defender."

"I'm sure working cases on an assembly line basis is disheartening at times, Drew. But PD's play a vital role in the system. Don't ever sell yourself short."

Charlie changed the subject. "What's your strategy for Ned's trial, David?"

"Whether or not the judge reduces the charge from first to second-degree murder we'll portray Ned as a sympathetic figure who was justified in killing the drug smuggler. If it looks like the jurors aren't likely to agree on an outright acquittal, our fallback position will be to argue Ned's only culpable of voluntary manslaughter and seek a probation only sentence."

"You might even have a slight chance of persuading a jury to let him walk. He had an absolute right to kill the Mexican smuggler. The catch is the means of the killing. Leaving him in the desert to die in agony will be quite an obstacle to overcome."

Jarrett said, "David leaps over trial obstacles the way Superman leaps over tall buildings."

"Then let's call him Super Lawyer."

I said, "I guess I'll have to charge our dinner to my kryptonite credit card instead of the platinum one."

CHAPTER THREE

Sunday morning Jarrett, Jim, and I ate breakfast in the hotel's café before driving out to the Federal Correctional Institution to see Ned.

The temperature was a hundred and three degrees, the winds were thirty-five to forty miles an hour, and claps of thunder and bolts of lightening accented the torrential rain pounding the city.

I felt secure in the sturdy Range Rover as I watched more conventional cars swaying in the strong winds and planning on the flooded roads.

But the weather wasn't deterring relatives and friends of prisoners from coming for a visit. They were lined up on the sidewalk in the downpour and trying to control their umbrellas as they waited to get into the visiting room's reception area.

Jarrett, Jim, and I were more fortunate. There was no line for the counsel's visiting room and we went straight to the entrance.

The bell was answered and the door unlocked by an attractive female officer. "Hi. Come in out of the storm. Which one of you is David Armstrong?"

I glanced at the nametag above one of her shapely breasts and said, "Good morning, Officer Collins. I'm David Armstrong. I made an appointment for my associates and me to see our client, Ned Johnson."

"You can call me, Kelly," she said as she ushered us to a three-sided cubicle containing a plastic table and chairs. "You're scheduled for an hour but if you finish earlier just give me a wave and I'll let you out. My desk is right over there."

Doing my best to ignore the sexual tension between Kelly and me, I thanked her.

An interior door opened and another officer brought Ned in. Ned was not tall but his bulky and muscular body gave him an imposing presence. His skin was copper-colored, his eyes were brown, and his hair was gleaming black.

I introduced him to Jarrett and Jim and we all took seats.

"How have you been since I last visited you, Ned?"

"As good as could be expected, David. I'm in a unit with other pre-trial detainees and they treat us more like guests than prisoners."

Jarrett said, "What do you think about the charges against you?"

"I don't feel what I did to the Mexican who killed my family was unreasonable. Something needed to be done to stop drug runners from rampaging through the reservation and destroying our *himdag*."

"What's *himdag*?"

"The Tohono O'odham customs, values, and way of life. The pot smugglers offer five thousand dollars just to drive their contraband to Phoenix. Many of our people, especially young men, accept the money not knowing stiff federal sentencing guidelines will subject them to years of imprisonment if they're apprehended. And those who refuse the money are often brutalized. I think that's what happened with my family but Chief Rivas tells me the drug runners coming through the rez now are real law-abiding knowing how the one I caught met his maker."

I said, "The U.S. Attorney overreacted to your actions. He indicted you for a crime that doesn't exist and tomorrow morning in court we'll ask the judge to reduce the charge to second-degree murder. We'll also ask the judge to assure you of a jury of your peers."

"I heard about your motions from my public defender."

"Why do juries in Pima County have so few Indians on them?"

"Jurors' names are mostly pulled from voter rolls and very few Tohono O'odhams participate in politics off the reservation. We're more interested in our tribal government. Then there's the problem of getting to court. Tucson is sixty to more than a hundred miles away depending on which part of the rez the people live on and many of them don't have cars."

"Thousands of Indians live and work in Tucson and many of them are members of your tribe so we'll insist the judge order the jury commissioner to add some Indians to the jury pool. On another subject, do you want us to negotiate a deal with the prosecutor for you to plead guilty to voluntary manslaughter? As a first-offender you'd qualify for a sentence as low as thirty-six months and be out of prison in around two years with time off for good behavior."

"No thanks. I'd rather you fight the murder charge. If I'm a convicted felon, I won't be eligible to keep my job with the police department."

"Fine by us, Ned. We're better fighters than negotiators anyway. Does Emily come to see you often?"

"Regular as clock works. She's a true friend. She was going to take some of the money she inherited from her grandfather to cover your fee until I told her you're helping me for nothing."

"Not exactly. The Project pays my salary and expenses. They also compensate Jarrett and Jim to assist me."

"Emily feels a lot of guilt over her bequest. Her great-grandfather made his fortune desecrating Mother Earth to extract minerals from Indian lands throughout the southwest, even from sacred sites."

"Then I'm glad we don't need any of her money. Do you have a suit to wear in court tomorrow?"

"Sears and Rareback's best, picked out by Emily herself in their Tucson store. She bought herself a new dress while she was there that makes her as pretty as a new penny."

Jim said, "I read somewhere that when a non-Indian woman is attracted to an Indian man she's said to have scarlet fever."

"You read right," said Ned with a chuckle. "And when an Indian man is hot for a non-Indian woman we say he's eating at the white man's trough."

We added our own chuckles and told Ned goodbye.

I tried and failed to not leer at the comely Kelly Collins as she let us out the front door.

The weather was still raging but visitors were no longer waiting on the sidewalk.

Jarrett, Jim, and I separated at the Radisson and agreed to meet in my suite for drinks at five.

I took a beer and a can of nuts out of the mini-bar and sat on the couch. Unable to free my mind of Officer Collins, I called my former father-in-law in hopes of getting an emotional tune-up from him.

Abe Davidson and I remained the best of friends despite my divorcing his daughter many years before.

His occupation was repairing cars out of the garage of his oceanfront home in Bodega Bay, California. His avocation was counseling people as a lay Adlerian analyst. Adler's daughter treated Abe when he was a young man stuck in a bad marriage and a bad job and he'd been a devotee of Adler's Theory of Individual Psychology ever since.

Following our greetings, Abe said, "You're probably not calling to pass the time of day, David. Tell me what your inner conflict is and I'll rub it and make it better."

"You always do. Everything's fine with my work and I wouldn't cheat on Felicia even if the world's sexiest supermodel begged me to bed her yet I got an erection when I met a female prison guard this morning."

"A blond with nice breasts?"

"Exactly."

"I've met her counterparts in many places and circumstances. We men are suckers for the blond and boobs combination even though studies show the women we end up with are usually opposite types. That's proved true in both of our lives. Don't be too tough on yourself, David. Penises have minds of their own."

"And personalities. I call mine Peter and I was so angry earlier I would've spanked him if I wasn't afraid he might like it and create more trouble for me than he already has."

"I'd love to do a paper on you and Peter for the *Adlerian Journal*. I wouldn't use your real name, of course."

"I can't imagine why anyone would find a fifty-five year old man with rampaging testosterone interesting but if you do, be my guest. You turned seventy-four in January, right?"

"Right."

"Do your still have rampaging testosterone?"

"I do, believe it or not. My urge to actually have sex is diminished but my fantasies are unabated. Young women dress very provocatively these days and I can't resist looking at them. I'm sure those who notice call me a dirty old man but I don't feel like an old man inside. I think all of us have an internal image of ourselves that is neither old nor young. We're simply the ageless us."

"I won't say you're a dirty old man then. I'll just say you're a dirty man of indeterminate age and thank you for keeping me mentally on track. I love you, Abe."

"I love you too, David."

Felicia's Marin County office manager lived with Abe and I asked him to give Marianne my regards before I said goodbye.

I found myself in the mood to talk on the phone and checked in with some of the other persons in my life.

My sister, JoAnne, was my biggest fan and faithfully followed my trials. I filled her in on my new case and she brought me up to date on my many nephews and nieces.

My next call was to my mentor, Melvin Berger. In his late eighties, Mel was still the most famous tort attorney on the globe and continuing to win huge awards for his clients.

During my very first trial I asked Mel for advice and he became a friend who helped me through the rough patches of my career.

One of the most important lessons he taught me was to treat every case as a crusade and be ruthless with anyone standing in the way of my client's freedom. Mel was such a fierce and relentless litigator you'd rather be locked in a room with a rabid Rottweiler than have him sue you.

I punched in the telephone number of Mel's Russian Hill home in San Francisco and his live-in chauffer and butler answered. "Good to hear from you, Prince David. Hold on a second and I'll get the Great Man for you."

In the background I heard Mel's bombastic voice say, "Tell the Prince the King's in the bathtub with a bimbo he picked up, Joshua. Tell him anything but get rid of him."

Mel then came on the phone. "Just messing with your mind, Youngster. Don't tell me you already need my assistance in that trial in Arizona."

"Not yet, thankfully."

"Well, if you do, I'm a patsy for American Indians. They got one of the rawest deals in history. Starting with the Pilgrims—whom some poet said fell first upon their knees and then upon the aborigines—and ending with the new nation's westward expansion, we did everything except eradicate all the native occupants of the land. I successfully defended Russell Means for leading the takeover of Alcatraz Island in the late sixties, you know. And my services were *pro bono*. The only other client I didn't bill in my long career was the Nob Hill Madam and she returned the favor by having her girls give me free nooky. Mules, tools, and fools work for nothing and I'm none of those. You're not calling to ask me for money, are you?"

"No, Mel. I'm simply taking advantage of a lull in my day to stay in touch with the persons I care about. You're high on my list."

"I'm sure the black fox is at the top. You and the Senator still an item?"

"Never more so and forever as far as I'm concerned."

Mel thanked me for the call but said he needed to hang up. "At my age, a commode and I are never far apart and I haven't been on mine for a few minutes."

My last call was to Felicia. She answered her cell phone in her car. "I'm on the way to a cocktail party at the French ambassador's residence. Pierre is one of the most charming and witty men in Washington."

"Is he married?"

"Oh yes, to a much better looking woman than me."

"I sincerely doubt that. Tell me what you're wearing."

"An above the knees purple dress with see-through sleeves."

"And your hair?"

"An up-do."

"High heels?"

"For sure."

"You'll be devoured by wolves, Nisha."

"My date will protect me."

"Your date?"

"James. He's my foreign affairs adviser. Don't be jealous. He's as gay as Jim is.

I'll talk to you again tomorrow. Think of me tonight."

"I'll think of James changing channels and having an irresistible impulse to paw you."

"It doesn't work that way, Darling. For the most part, people's sexual predispositions are hardwired."

I was switching from a beer to a scotch on the rocks when the desk phone rang and the caller said, "This is Thomas Sloan, the U.S. Attorney for Arizona, Mr. Armstrong. Do you have a moment to speak with me?"

"Go ahead."

"You've got us behind the eight ball on the motion to quash the indictment. There's no way around the fact we goofed up and to avoid as much embarrassment as possible I'd like to arrange a deal with you before tomorrow's court session."

"What do you have in mind?" I asked, amused at his use of the pronoun "we" to cover his tracks.

"We'll withdraw the flawed indictment and file a charge of second-degree murder by complaint only if you'll agree to waive an evidentiary hearing."

"I'll need to speak with my client. How can I reach you?

"Call me on my direct line," he said and gave me the number.

I was relieved the guard who answered the telephone at the federal prison wasn't Officer Collins.

He was just as friendly and accommodating, though, and I was soon talking to Ned.

I repeated what Sloan told me and Ned said, "What will we lose if we give up the evidentiary hearing?"

"Nothing. The purpose of such hearings is for a judge to determine if the prosecution has enough evidence to establish probable cause. In your case, we know they do. Another factor to consider is the reduced charge isn't a capital punishment crime so you'd be eligible for release from pre-trial confinement."

"Then let's accept the big chief's offer. I'll sleep a lot better tonight now that I'm no longer staring at a death sentence and might even breathe fresh air again soon. I don't know what you did to make this happen, David. I sure am grateful, though."

Sloan answered his direct line on the first ring and I said, "We're agreeable to your proposition under one condition, Mr. Sloan. We want you and your assistant prosecutors to not object to my request for Ned's discharge from custody. Under the new charge he's eligible for release on his own recognizance."

"You drive a hard bargain but we have a deal. Don't think this means we won't still strive to put Johnson away for a long, long time, Mr. Armstrong. The administrative glitch on the indictment was an anomaly. We're making sure all our T's are crossed and our I's dotted from here on out."

"How did you know I was in the Radisson, Mr. Sloan?"

"From the front page article on you in today's *Tucson Star*. Thanks for your cooperation, sir. Good day."

I picked up the copy of the newspaper I found outside my door that morning.

Beneath a photograph of me coming down the stairs of my Beech Premier was a piece by a reporter:

> Yesterday the prominent and widely heralded trial attorney, David Armstrong, piloted his private jet into Tucson airport with his defense team and checked into the downtown Radisson Suites.
>
> Mr. Armstrong recently made international news by defending Charles Manson in a sensational retrial. Mr. Armstrong is the executive director of the Innocent Prisoners Project, an organization in New York dedicated to exonerating wrongfully incarcerated prisoners. Founded in the mid-nineties, the Project has since freed more than four hundred falsely convicted persons, many of them from death rows in states around the country, including Arizona.
>
> Mr. Armstrong also takes on cases he finds interesting and tomorrow morning in federal Judge Vaughn Warren's courtroom he will represent Ned Johnson, the Tohono O'odham tribal police officer accused of torturing to death a Mexican drug smuggler he says killed his parents and raped and killed his sister.
>
> Prior to coming to Tucson Mr. Armstrong filed motions to quash the indictment and to have his client tried by a jury with more Indians than are in the current Pima County jury pool. Briefs in support of the latter motion were filed by preeminent legal experts such as the Dean of the University of Arizona law school, the head of the State Bar Association, and the Chief Justice of the Arizona Supreme Court, among others.

High-powered counsels such as Mr. Armstrong are a rarity here and a large turnout of reporters and spectators is expected in Judge Warren's court on Monday.

When Jarrett and Jim came to the suite I informed them of the deal with Sloan and showed them the article.

Jim said, "Maybe this is why one of your fans is here. The female prison guard you were making eyes at this morning is in the downstairs bar hoping you'll join her. I'm not attracted to members of the opposite sex but for those who are she's looking good in a skimpy dress. If we hadn't been the sole of discretion when she asked us for your room number, she'd be scratching her nails on your door now."

"Then let's have our drinks down there and I'll confront her head on."

"I think she might have mentioned the word head," Jim said.

Jarrett snickered and said he had a similar recollection as we stepped into an elevator.

From her stool at the bar Kelly Collins saw us enter and take a table.

She strode over and said, "Hi, David. I was telling Jarrett and Jim I hoped you'd come down and here you are. May I sit?"

"Please do."

"I'm not usually so forward but I attend law school at night and my criminal procedures professor has been talking about you and the upcoming trial. When you arrived at the prison this morning I felt like I was meeting a movie star and after my shift was over I decided I had try to get to know you better."

"I'm flattered by your interest, Kelly. The problem is I'm involved in a long-term monogamous romance with a woman back east and being seen in the company of another female, especially one as attractive as you, while I'm in a hotel three thousand miles away could endanger our relationship."

"It's not like I'm trying to seduce you, David."

"Appearances can be misinterpreted, Kelly."

"I'm sorry I bothered you," she said then got up and hurried out of the bar.

"You handled the situation very well," Jarrett said.

"I thought a brutally frank approach was best under the circumstances. The fact she's drawn to an unreal image of me from the publicity is why she's a distraction instead of an ego boost. I imagine her law professor depicted me as a heroic paladin riding into town to right injustice."

Through the windows we saw the rain still falling so after second drinks we went into the restaurant next to the bar for dinner.

The daily special of coconut shrimp with black bean cakes appealed to all three of us and the dish turned out to be as good as it sounded.

CHAPTER FOUR

The storm moved out during the night and the local weather forecast for Monday was sunny skies with a temperature of a hundred and five degrees.

Jarrett, Jim, and I once again met for breakfast in the lobby café then went to the federal courthouse in the Land Rover with the air conditioner on full blast.

We parked in the basement garage, took an elevator to the fifth floor, and several reporters in the hallway posed questions for me until I held up a hand. "I'll try to save us from going through this exercise every day by saying I never make public comments about a case during a trial. I take seriously my responsibility under the Bar's code of professional conduct to refrain from making extrajudicial statements that might taint potential jurors or otherwise materially prejudice the proceeding. If you still have questions after this contest has been decided, I'll talk to you then."

The reporters begrudgingly let us pass and we went inside Judge Warren's courtroom. The building was fairly new and I found the modern furnishings and blond wood-paneling of the space an inferior contrast to the majestic chambers still in use around the country in older federal structures.

However, the cutting-edge technology installed in the courtroom was a welcome improvement. The surrounding speaker system would enable trial participants and spectators to clearly hear all communications. And video monitors were mounted on counsels' tables, the witness stand, the bench, the clerk's desk, and throughout the jury box.

We put our laptops and attaches on the defense table and a young woman stepped forward. "Good morning, David. I'm Emily Crenshaw, Ned's girlfriend. We met when you came to see Ned several months ago. Do you remember?"

"Yes, of course, Emily. Good to see you again. These are my associates, Jarrett and Jim."

They shook hands with her and I said, "Take one of the chairs on the first row bench here. Ned will be in soon and I'm sure he'll welcome the sight of you."

"He called me last night and said the judge may let him go home today. Do you think the judge really will?"

"Very possibly, Emily," I said and her face flushed with anticipation.

A group of three people entered and came to a stop at the defense table.

The man said, "I'm Doug Axelrod and these legal whiz-bangs are Linda Metcalf who's assisting me, and Kaya Kabotie, our boss."

We introduced ourselves in kind and Axelrod presented me with a fat file folder. "This is the discovery I promised, Mr. Armstrong. I'm pleased to meet all of you."

They sat at the prosecution table next to us and a few minutes before nine two U.S. Marshals brought Ned in through a rear door.

He and Emily were embracing over the railing when the bailiff called for order and Judge Warren took the bench.

My heart sank at the sight of his appearance. The squinty, mean eyes and down-turned corners of his mouth were clear body language of a stern, impatient man cemented in his ways.

Foregoing any pleasantries, he said, "Counsels, state your names for the record."

"Douglas Axelrod and Linda Metcalf for the Government, Your Honor. Kaya Kabotie, the supervisor of the Tucson branch of the U.S. Attorney's office, is sitting in for today's hearing."

"David Armstrong, Jarrett Hudson, and James Brown for the defense, Your Honor."

"The Court is in receipt of three motions from the defense which ..."

Axelrod rose. "Your Honor, pardon me for interrupting but I have an announcement that will render one of those motions moot. The Government concedes the indictment for first-degree murder-torture was incorrectly drawn."

He dropped some papers on our table, left another set with the clerk, and continued. "We're filing a complaint of second-degree murder to correct our mistake. The defense has agreed to waive an evidentiary hearing so the defendant can be arraigned on the new charge without delay."

The judge looked my way and I said, "Mr. Axelrod's representation is correct, Your Honor. We waive a probable cause hearing."

"Very well," he said, reaching down to receive a copy of the complaint from his clerk. "The defendant will rise."

Ned complied and Judge Warren said, "Mr. Johnson, I dismiss the original indictment and re-arraign you for second-degree murder, which carries a maximum sentence of life imprisonment. Do you understand the charge and the potential punishment?"

"Yes, sir."

"How do you plea to the new charge?"

"Not guilty."

You may resume your seat."

I said, "Your Honor, now that Lieutenant Johnson is no longer accused of a capital offense his continued confinement is not required under the Federal Bail Reform Act. He's never been convicted of any crime, he has long-term ties to the Tohono O'odham reservation where he is a command-level officer in the police department, and he's not a flight risk or a danger to the community. I ask you to release him on his own recognizance."

"Mr. Axelrod?"

"We have no objection to the defense's request, Your Honor."

"Mr. Johnson, I order you released on your own recognizance. When you're processed out of the prison's detention unit you'll be provided a form to read and sign. The form will outline the conditions you must abide by under this release. Violate any of them and you'll find yourself right back behind bars."

"I understand, sir. Thank you."

"No thanks due. My decision was based on the law, not on any favor for you. I'll next address the defense's discovery motion."

Axelrod said, "We delivered the discovery to them this morning and I gave the court's copies to your clerk."

"You're making my job easy, Mr. Axelrod. Shall I ask for debate on the defense's motion for a more diverse jury or have you already settled that issue too?"

"We have not."

"Mr. Armstrong, I'll hear oral argument in support of the brief."

"Your Honor and opposing counsels, the Supreme Court of the United States has long recognized a defendant's Sixth Amendment right to be tried by an impartial jury selected from a venire constituted of a fair cross-section of the community. The defense team's client is a Tohomo O'odham Indian and if he's tried by jurors selected from this district's current federal jury pool, he'll be deprived of his constitutional guarantee to be tried by a jury of his peers. Not a single member of his tribe or from any other tribe in the area is in the jury pool. This, despite the fact that there are more than thirty thousand American Indians residing in the county. When I asked the jury commissioner why none were in the pool she told me they mostly live on remote reservations without mailing addresses. Her excuse ignores the many Indians residing within the city limits of Tucson.

"In their nineteen sixty-seven decision in Jones v. Georgia the United States Supreme Court definitively dealt with the problem of racially imbalanced juries by holding that the fair cross-section requirement was a fundamental right. I quote: 'The purpose of a diverse jury is to guard against bias and the exercise of arbitrary power and make available the commonsense judgment of the community as a hedge against the overzealous or mistaken prosecutor and in preference to the professional or over-conditioned response of a judge. This prophylactic protection is not provided if the jury pool is made up of only certain segments of the populace and other groups are excluded from participation.' End quote.

"The Court's subsequent decision in Duren v. Missouri established a three-prong analytical approach to determine whether the fair cross-section requirement of Jones was violated. To sustain Duren claims defendants must prove the group alleged to be excluded is a distinctive group in the community; prove the representation of the group in jury pools is not fair and reasonable in relation to the total number of persons in the community; and prove the under-representation is due to systematic exclusion of the minority group in the jury selection process.

"All the federal appellate panels that have heard Duren claims have conceded the first two prongs but denied the claims on the ground that the systematic exclusion prong was not met. In my opinion, these claims were lost because the lawyers making them forgot about the prior precedent opinion in Jones, which holds that a fourteen percent or higher disparity between the excluded group's population in a community and their representation on a community's jury is *prima facia* discrimination. Since the disparity between Indians living in this county and their representation on the master jury roll is almost seventeen percent the defense relies on Jones and rests our case."

"Does the prosecution wish to rebut?"

Kaya Kabotie stood. "No, Your Honor. We support the defense's motion. As a Hopi I've been concerned about the lack of Indians on our juries for some time. Without accusing the jury commissioner of a concerted effort to exclude Indians from jury service, I think she's been lax in her duties and should be ordered to use her subpoena power to insure greater participation in the judicial process by Pima County Native Americans."

"Are you speaking personally or in your capacity as supervising officer of the local U.S. Attorney's office?"

"Both and with the full knowledge and approval of the U.S. Attorney for the Arizona district, Your Honor."

"Anything further, Mr. Armstrong?"

"No, Your Honor."

"I'll take the motion under consideration and issue my ruling at next Monday's first preliminary hearing. Until then we'll proceed as scheduled. Mindful of the need for counsels to gain information about potential jurors in order to challenge their qualifications to serve, I've arranged for each side to have copies of the questionnaires the one-hundred members of the federal pool filled out. You can pick them up from my clerk on your way out today. I'm also mindful of the jury candidates' privacy concerns so on your copies their addresses and telephone numbers have been erased. I'll exercise my discretion and be the sole questioner in *voir dire*. The only role you lawyers will play is making your challenges. Court is adjourned until nine a.m. July 18th."

Ned clasped my hand so firmly I almost winced. "I owe you, David. You ever need anything just ask."

"I'm only doing my job, Ned. What's the first thing you'll do when you get out?"

"Burn some sage buds in my family's house and do a ceremony to get rid of the evil spirits. Then I'll take Emily to my trailer and cook us a meal of tepary beans, rice, sweet corn, tomatoes, and tortillas."

The two U.S. Marshals made their presence known and took Ned away after Emily told him she'd wait at the prison and drive him to the reservation when he was released.

I walked over to the prosecution's table. "Ms. Kabotie, I appreciate you going further than you needed to in support of our motion. I'm sure Mr. Sloan would've preferred you not being so enthusiastic."

"My conscience wouldn't permit anything less. I have great respect for the organization you manage, Mr. Armstrong, and I'd like to have a chat with you after this trial is over if you're amenable."

"It will be my pleasure, Ms. Kabotie."

"It's Mrs. Kabotie but Kaya will do."

"And I'm David."

Jarrett and Jim picked up our copies of the jury questionnaires while I was talking to Kaya so we left with each of them carrying fifty questionnaires and me carrying the file-full of discovery documents.

At the hotel we stopped in the business center to have the questionnaires scanned into my laptop and when we went to my suite I emailed them to Jarrett and Jim; and to Cheryl in the New York office.

We ordered sandwiches from room service and ate them as we began reading the questionnaires and taking notes.

Jim finished chewing the last bite of his grilled chicken sub and said, "When I've gone through all these forms I'll run background checks on the candidates. The court clerk blocking out their addresses and phone numbers doesn't matter. She left their social security numbers in. This will be an ongoing project because I want to go out to the reservation tomorrow and start my investigation."

"The Land Rover is yours to use," I said, tossing him the keys. "I'll hole up here reading about the jury candidates and examining the prosecution's evidence."

Jarrett said, "I'll help you."

CHAPTER FIVE

Tuesday morning Jim departed for the reservation and Jarrett and I met in my suite to continue assessing the jury candidates.

By lunch time we were done and we strolled in hundred-plus heat to a nearby restaurant to indulge in New York style pizzas and microbrews before returning to the suite.

I emptied the file folder of discovery on the coffee table between Jarrett between me and we arranged the documents in the order of Axelrod's likely presentation.

A statement by Jesse Rivas, Chief of the Tohono O'odham Police Department, regarding Ned's informal confession was first. The written account of the FBI agent in charge of the case who took Ned into federal custody and videotaped him saying why and how he'd killed the Mexican drug smuggler was next in line. The last three sets of papers were the report of the FBI's evidence response team leader; an FBI crime lab supervisor's summary of the test results on evidence gathered from the crimes scenes; and the findings of a Pima County Deputy Medical Examiner who performed autopsies on the Johnson family victims and the Mexican drug smuggler.

Leafing through the documents, I said, "The deputy medical examiner couldn't determine if the Mexican's death was caused by the rifle shot to his abdomen or the eating of his lungs and heart by wild animals."

"Maybe we should send the autopsy report to Doc Shapiro for a second opinion?"

"Good idea." Dr. Philip Shapiro was a renowned forensic pathology expert I often retained in trials. "I'll be back as soon as I go down to the Business Center to make a copy of the ME's report and FedEx it to the doc."

On my return to the suite Jarrett said, "A witness we should put some heat on is the FBI agent, Dale Watson. Scraping blood samples off Ned's boots after he arrested him was an illegal search. And asking Ned to admit how long he took to stake out the Mexican in the desert was a smarmy attempt to negate a killing in the heat of passion assertion."

"You're right. I'll have Jim find out what infraction caused Watson to be transferred to no man's land as the lone agent to investigate crimes on the Tohono O'odham reservation. Talk about ending up at the bottom of the totem pole."

Jim called in the late afternoon to let us know he wouldn't be having dinner with us. "Chief Rivas gave me a tour of the reservation today that produced lots of leads to explore so I'll stay out here a couple more days. He's letting me use the air-conditioned and furnished trailer he lived in behind police headquarters until he got married. Anything new on your end?"

"Not much. Jarrett and I finished going through the questionnaires and the prosecution's evidence. So far there are only five witnesses on their list—Chief Rivas; the FBI agent in charge of the investigation; the leader of the FBI's evidence response team; an FBI crime lab supervisor; and a county medical examiner. I emailed their names to you and I'd like you to check them out, especially the FBI agent. I'm interested in knowing how he came to be transferred to Tucson and assigned to the lowly duty of handling crimes on the Tohono O'odham reservation."

"Will do. I brought my laptop with me and I'll check the witnesses out in my borrowed abode tonight."

"Sorry about you having to withdraw from scotch while you're out there."

"Worry not. I bought a bottle at a liquor store before leaving Tucson this morning."

We didn't hear from Jim again until late Thursday afternoon when he phoned to say he was on his way back to the hotel and craving meat.

"Do you want to go to McMahon's Steak House again?" I asked.

"A barbecue joint would be better."

"I'll see which ones are considered the best in town. Come to my suite when you get here and we'll discuss the options over drinks."

Upon Jim's arrival I poured him a scotch and said, "Okay, great white scout, brief us on your expedition into Injun country."

"First of all, the land is breathtaking and seemingly endless. The drive from Tucson to Sells, the reservation's main town where the tribe's headquarters, the police department, a few businesses, and a hospital are, took me an hour, and it was another hour to Ned's trailer and his family's house. Chief Rivas took me out there in his Toyota 4Runner. He told me he only has twenty cops a shift to patrol three-million acres on an area roughly the size of Connecticut stretching across three Arizona counties. Plus his cops don't have jurisdiction over non-Indians and can't directly deal with problem of Mexican drug smugglers so the reservation is overrun with law enforcement personnel from the Border Patrol, DEA, deputy sheriffs, and the State highway patrol. There's also a company of National Guard soldiers and even a small contingent of CIA spooks operating surveillance drones. Despite all those resources Riva estimates they're only seizing a small percentage of the billions of dollars of pot being brought in every year."

Jarrett said, "Ned gave us the impression the smugglers were daunted by the way he killed the one he caught in his parent's house."

"Rivas may've been trying to make Ned feel better but he told me the drugs keep coming in. His take on the crisis is that since the smugglers are sent by ruthless Sinaloa Drug Cartel bosses they know if they don't sell their pot and return with the money, their families will be killed. So he sees them as men who will go to any length to achieve their objective."

I said, "Sounds like you and Rivas got along well."

"We bonded over my bottle of scotch in the trailer he loaned me. By the way, trailers, adobe huts, and slanted roof lean-tos are the main types of dwellings on the reservation. There are also some newer HUD modular houses but many Tohono O'odham shun them for being non-traditional."

"Did you get a chance to speak with Emily Crenshaw?"

"I did—once with Ned present and once without him. He's moved into Emily's apartment in Sells but she told me she wasn't pushing for marriage while he's facing the trial. Although she's mousy in appearance, an inner beauty glows when she's with Ned or talking about him. He dotes on Emily too and is impressed with the life she chose to lead despite the inheritance of what he calls blood money. TOCA, the community action organization she formed, has been successful with their food program and they've started a co-op for the women basket-weavers to sell their products at local markets and fairs. Emily also created an outreach project to Tohono O'odham elders to keep everyone, especially the younger children, invested in keeping the tribe's traditions alive."

Jim flipped to a page on his notebook and continued. "Some of the younger generation has gone the opposite direction. Last night I saw a flyer advertising a concert at the rodeo arena by a reservation band named S-Cuk Gogs and I went to hear them. They're a combination heavy metal and punk rock group with a big racial chip on their shoulders. Here are the lyrics to one of their songs.

He played a recording on his lap top and we heard:

> We're so happy to be putted on a reservation.
> We were born on this institution land.
> You sent our forefathers here at gunpoint.
> Are you amazed at what's left of our culture?
> Our hills are covered with Thunderbird bottles
> and the smell of puke and shit is enough to
> make you mad at your spiritual leader for pissing
> his pants.
>
> We're so glad to be putted on a reservation.
> We're so happy to be part of a foreign system.
> We're so happy to be living off government products
> while alcohol, diabetes and suicide wipe us out.
> We're so happy to be putted on a reservation.

And this is their anti-tourist song:

> Do you injuns still live in teepees?
> Why don't you have feathers in your hair?
> Do you still use bows and arrows?
> Are you going to do a forbidden dance for us?
>
> Why do you have regular names instead of ones with color in them?
> Are you heavy smokers?
> I heard you were heavy drinkers.
>
> Why don't you get your eyes away from the TV screen, idiots?
> We may be injuns but we don't come from no John Wayne flick.

I asked what the mood of the crowd was and Jim said, "Radically pro-Indian. As one of the very few white people in attendance, I felt like a missionary who'd been invited for dinner and wondering if maybe I was dinner. To give a balanced report, I have to say Emily told me most of the other reservation bands perform *Waila*, the 'happy dance' music of the Tohono O'odham. She says the most popular group is Gertie and the T.O. Boyz.

"Moving right along, Chief Rivas is forwarding us a record of all the attacks by drug smugglers on reservation residents. He's also forwarding us the info he has on Fabian Ruiz, the smuggler Ned killed. Ruiz was a known member of the Sinaloa Cartel with a long police record and confinement for offenses from robbery to murder. He received the maximum fifty-year sentence in his last trial—Mexico doesn't impose life imprisonment or the death penalty for any crime—but the cartel broke Ruiz and scores of other inmates out of prison only a month before he met his fate in the Sonoran Desert at the hands of Ned. Lastly, I ran checks on the prosecution witnesses. Chief Rivas is squeaky clean as is the leader of the FBI evidence response team. The FBI crime lab supervisor can be discredited by our usual attack on the lab's credibility. And the county medical examiner blew an autopsy in 2007 that forced the DA to drop charges against a murder suspect. I emailed Jarrett and you the details. Here's the skinny on FBI Special Agent Dale Watson. In his previous assignment in New Orleans he was suspected of revealing the identity of a confidential informant to a mobster facing trial. The informant's mutilated and dismembered body was found in a French Quarter dumpster the next day and the prosecution of the mobster couldn't proceed. There was no proof Watson leaked the informant's secret location to the mob but the Bureau brass still needed to put him somewhere out of the public eye so they sent him to be the Indian affairs agent in Tucson, their equivalent of a Siberian assignment. Now let's talk *carne!*"

"Why are you feeling so deprived of flesh?"

"The damned community action organization Emily started has made meat as scarce on the reservation as legally bottled booze. Tohono O'odham's have the highest rate of diabetes in the world and she and her fellow TOCA board members are encouraging them to give up fatty and sweet foods in favor of a traditional diet. TOCA runs the Desert Rain Café, the only restaurant in Sells, and I'll be glad if I never eat another bean or cactus product as long as I live. I'm way beyond ready for some barbecue. Where can we get some?"

"I couldn't find any consensus on the best barbeque restaurants in Tucson but a chef who was driving through recommends Mr. K's in the south side of town. The chef describes the place as a hole in the wall with no ambience but says the hickory-smoked meat with a spicy, spicy, spicy sauce is the best in the country except for a joint in North Little Rock, Arkansas."

"Take me there at once."

"There's a downside. South Tucson is a high-crime area with frequent clashes between black and Mexican gangs."

"I'm armed and dangerous. The 30.6 Remington rifle I bought will down an elk at five hundred yards so I expect it's capable of ruining the day of a hoodlum or two as well."

We didn't need the Land Rover's GPS system to pinpoint Mr. K's. The aroma from the barbecue pit led us directly to the street corner the building was on as if we were drawn by a magnet.

The dining area was also used for storage and the unmatched tables and chairs looked like they were bought at successive yard sales. But the pork ribs all three of us ordered were special. So were the side dishes of ranch beans, turnip greens, okra, slaw and cornbread. The sweet potato pie dessert also went down easily.

We thanked the man in overalls at the counter and asked if he was Mr. K.

"No, sir. I'm the manager. Mr. Kendrick puts all his time in his Afro-American Museum next door. Take a peek before you leave."

We followed the manager's suggestion and were impressed by the collection of memorabilia of Black life in Tucson in the 40's through the 60's. In a photograph of Mr. K's restaurant developed in April, 1953 a sign over the front door read TAKE OUT ONLY. And separate windows were shown for blacks and whites to pick up their orders.

A delightful experience was Mr. K's and one we would repeat regularly during our stay in Tucson.

CHAPTER SIX

Friday morning at breakfast I asked Jarrett if he thought an interlocutory appeal of Judge Warren's order denying our motion for Indian representation on the jury was warranted.

"Off the top of my head, yes. I'll see whether the case law on the subject has changed since I last checked and give you a more definitive answer later."

"If you determine an appeal is viable, go ahead and prepare one. And Jim, you still have to read the juror questionnaires so let's all work separately the rest of the day and get together in my suite for drinks at five."

I called my office and asked Cheryl if she received the file of juror questionnaires I sent her.

"Yes. Using the information on the form I created a spreadsheet listing the pool member's names, sex, age, date of birth, place of birth, marital status, children, education, occupation, military experience, and membership in organizations. I added three other categories—crime victim history, law enforcement history, and police record. When Jim copies me on his background reports I'll fill those categories in and transmit the spreadsheet to you."

"You're a big help, Cheryl. Are you still involved with the Italian Stallion sports bar owner on Staten Island?"

"More than ever. We have the same appetites for sex and food, which is to say we both like both a lot. The only small problem we have is my snobbishness. As a born and bred Manhattan woman I can't help looking down on Staten Island. I hope he continues to think I'm only kidding."

"How do you rate Will's performance?"

"I give him a B-plus. If I weren't jealous because I'm the person who's really in charge when you aren't here, I might even up the grade to an A-minus. You want to talk to him?"

"Please Ms. *de facto* assistant executive director."

Will came on the line. I listened to his report, advised him on how to handle a delicate situation, reminded him to call me on my cell phone anytime he needed to, and asked him to transfer my call to Burt and Arthur's office.

I briefed them on Ned's case and they brought me up to date on the Project then I turned on my laptop and composed a motion for Judge Warren to exercise his discretion to allow Axelrod and me to examine the jury candidate after him during *voir dire*. I figured the motion would have merit even if we didn't file an interlocutory appeal so I emailed it to the court and the prosecutor then went for a pipe smoking walk in the neighborhood.

The temperature was "only" ninety-nine degrees and a blustery wind was blowing the skirts of coeds from the nearby university so I stayed outside until the heat forced me to return to the air-conditioned comfort of the Radisson.

Following a light lunch and a cold beer I whiled away the afternoon thinking of affirmative defense tactics and listing people other than Ned I might want to put on the stand.

Jarrett, Jim, and I reconvened in my suite for drinks at five and Jarrett said, "An interlocutory appeal is a go. The Supreme Court upheld the right as recently as last December. I copied you on the brief I wrote."

"You're the appellate specialist, Jarrett. I don't need to check your work. Send off the final version and be prepared to argue our position on Monday."

"Okay. I've also been researching affirmative defenses to homicide and after reading all the relevant Supreme Court and Ninth Circuit cases I believe the only problem we'll face in asserting the killing by Ned was justified will be overcoming the Government's contention that leaving the Mexican man staked out in the desert to be attacked by wild animals was unreasonable force."

"The Government will have to prove the man was alive during the attacks and their medical examiner can't say if he died from the gunshot wound or the evisceration of his lungs and heart by the animals."

Jim asked why it wasn't up to us to prove the force was justified and I said, "Under Ninth Circuit law all we have to do is raise the affirmative defense. The prosecution must disprove the defense beyond a reasonable doubt. If they can't and the jurors are fair, they won't be able to find Ned guilty of murder."

"You have an unrealistic expectation of fairness. The outcomes of federal trials are as preordained as the Spanish Inquisition hearings were."

Jarrett said, "Of course the contest is slanted in favor of the Government, Jim. But we can't win if we don't try."

I asked Jim how the investigation of the jury pool members was coming and he said, "We'll know soon. Richard's using our powerful office computer to run background reports on them."

"Thanks for your efforts, Partners. Since we're ahead of the curve you two are welcome to fly home for the weekend if you'd like."

"No way," Jim said. "As always, we're with you from the start to the finish of a trial."

Jarrett concurred. "You once told us we're like a football team preparing for a big game. We can't let sex distract us from our goal."

"Then let's call it a day and drive out to the reservation. I want to try the Indian food café Jim liked so much."

Jim frowned. "You can go without me. I'd rather force down a dog turd sandwich than eat there again."

"Suggest a more palatable cuisine and Jarrett and I may stay and dine with you."

"Mexican."

His choice was accepted by acclamation and after an internet search for "the most authentic Mexican restaurant in Tucson" we found ourselves back on the South side of town. El Indio's décor was drab, our waitress spoke very little English, and we were among the very few *gringo* customers but the enchiladas, tamales, tacos with green and red chili sauces were flavorful and zesty.

Jarrett and Susan, Jim and Richard, and Abe and Marianne, were frequent guests of the Puerto Vallarta condominium Felicia and I co-owned and Jim said, "I wonder why the food we eat in PV isn't as good as this?"

I said, "For most people in that particular area of Mexico lunch or dinner is usually a plate of fish, meat, or poultry with rice, beans, and vegetables. What we're eating is snack food to them which they don't prepare with the succulent sauces and care cooks up here do. However, the Mexican States of Oaxaca, Veracruz, and Yucatan, for instance, have elevated snack food to an art form."

Jarrett munched on his tamale and said, "I'm glad at least some people in Mexico are eating mouthfuls of goodness like these. They're sinfully delicious."

As soon as I was back in my suite I phoned Felicia to run an idea by her. She enthusiastically signed off on my whimsical plan so I took the next step and also got commitments from Susan and Richard, Jarrett's and Jim's respective lovers. Booking accommodations for all of us was the only remaining task and the internet made that easy.

I then called Jarrett and Jim and asked them to come see me for a moment.

They showed up and Jim said, "What's up, Boss? Did you receive a flash of brilliance you want to share or are you laying us off?"

"Neither. We're ready for Monday's hearing so let's have a relaxing weekend.

Where I'm taking us is a surprise. All you need do is pack an overnight bag with two days of casual clothes and meet me downstairs for breakfast at seven in the morning ready to go."

They both smiled and saluted.

I reciprocated and said, "Company dismissed."

The prospect of being with Felicia the next day kept me awake for awhile but I eventually fell asleep looking at my favorite picture of her in a sleeveless, black cocktail dress with welcoming eyes fixed only on me. The actual photograph was on the bedside table in the master stateroom of my boat but the image was forever imprinted in my mind thus always available for viewing wherever I happened to be.

Saturday I rose in time to watch a multi-colored sunrise before going down to the café.

Jarrett and Jim prodded me to reveal our weekend plans and I partially relented. "We'll end up at the Grand Canyon after an aerial tour of the reservation and a mystery stop in Phoenix."

My freshly washed Beechcraft Premier was out of the hangar and waiting for us in front of the Executive Terminal at Tucson's airport. I climbed aboard first in order to start the engines and turn on the air-conditioning to combat the stifling heat.

Jim took the co-pilot's seat and Jarrett sat behind him in a pull-down chair.

I told a tower controller I would be flying under visual flight rules and he cleared me for takeoff and gave me permission to fly through two restricted air zones over the Tohono O'odham reservation.

We were there quickly and looking down on land as foreboding and alien as the moon's surface.

The sunlight was glinting off rock formations on Baboquivari Peak and Jarrett said, "How high is that mountain?"

"The chart indicates a little over seven thousand feet. The Tohono O'odham people believe their creator lives in a cave at the base of the peak."

I circled the area twice then set a course for Phoenix.

Twenty-seven minutes later we landed at the city's Sky Harbor Airport and were directed to Cutter Aviation's general aviation facility.

The sight of Richard and Susan standing outside the waiting room grinning and waving at us dispelled any surprise.

I parked the jet and shut down the engines and followed Jarrett and Jim down the boarding stairs.

Once Susan and Jarrett were finished embracing she said, "Felicia's plane landed a few minutes ago, David. She called me from the terminal and said United VIP staff members were bringing her here."

Sure enough, a car bearing the airline's logo soon appeared and Felicia and I got our turn to kiss and embrace. She was six feet tall but the two inch heels she wore brought our lips level—and our groins. If the two United employees were embarrassed by our physical display of affection for each other, they didn't show it.

When we finally let each other go one of them said, "Will there be anything else, Senator Bates-Baxter?"

"Not for now, thanks, but remind your supervisor I'll need a ride from here to my terminal Sunday afternoon at five."

"Someone will attend to you need without fail, Senator. Have a nice weekend."

Jarrett and Susan and Jim and Richard were content to sit side by side in the passenger cabin so Felicia took the co-pilot's chair. With skin and eyes as black as an African night, teeth as white as a Snowy Egret's feathers, a figure as pleasing as Venus's, and features as becoming as Aphrodite's, Mrs. Bate's brainy, accomplished daughter was quite a sight. In fact, she was so alluring in her curve-clinging sheath I had to restrain myself from closing the cockpit door and pouncing on her.

Instead, I restarted the turbines, let the tower know I was ready to leave, and a controller cleared me for immediate take-off on a runway not being used by arriving and departing airliners.

I climbed to fifteen-thousand feet, activated the auto-pilot, and took Felicia's hand. "I'm so glad you could get away, Nisha. Did you have to cancel any engagements?"

"Only an interview with a *Washington Post* reporter running down the rumor I'm burned out on the political process. I told her my denial on the phone would have to suffice. One lesson I've learned in my years of service in the Capitol is that situations always change—sometimes for the better, sometimes for the worst—but they always change. Right now they're about as bad as I've ever seen them but I'm not a quitter and I'll do everything in my power to prevent the closet racists in Congress and the media from preventing the first black President in our history a chance to deliver on his promise of change for America."

"Are you suggesting he should be immune from criticism because he's black?" I gently chided.

"Not as long as the criticism is fair and free of color bias. The two-party system in American politics only works if the opposing party members are honorable. Too many of today's Republicans are closet rednecks who secretly drape themselves in the Confederate flag and long for the reinstitution of slavery."

"Here, here," I said, clapping.

I radioed the tower at Grand Canyon Airport when we're ten miles out and was cleared for a long straight-in landing on the lengthy north-south runway.

The jet's wheels squeaked onto the tarmac and I taxied to Grand Canyon Airways office. They also provided services to private aircraft and in return for the jet fuel I purchased, overnight parking in a hangar was free, as was a van ride to the Lodge, the only Government run hotel in the national park.

I chose the Lodge because it was on the north rim which was a thousand feet higher than the south rim and cooler. And also because almost all the camera-snapping tourists gravitated to the south rim so the grand old hotel was in a more secluded area.

The rim-view rooms I reserved were rustic with timbered ceilings, pine floors and walls but more than adequate for our needs. And the view from the balconies was unparalleled.

When we all eschewed group activity in favor of meeting for early evening drinks in the Roughrider Saloon Felicia and I locked our door and disrobed as frantically as any other couple anxious for an afternoon tryst.

Following a passionate interlude in bed we redressed, shared a sandwich in the hotel restaurant, and hiked on a self-guided trail to Bright Angel Point where we saw and heard the Roaring Springs three-thousand feet below us.

We met Jarrett, Susan, Jim, and Richard in the saloon at six and they appeared as contented with themselves as we were.

While we enjoyed our drinks we discussed dinner options for the evening and recreation options for the next day and reached agreement on going to the Chuck Wagon for our night's food and being at the Kaibab Trailhead at seven-thirty Sunday morning for mule rides into the canyon.

The Chuck Wagon was literally an old trail cooking wagon. We sat at makeshift tables around an open pit fire and were served briskets of bison with skewered potatoes and onions, baked beans, and biscuits on tin plates. Before portions of peach cobbler were brought out we were also offered mountain oysters. Responding to our inquiries, the waiter said they were calf's testicles coated in buttermilk and flour and deep fried—a staple of the American cowboy diet in the latter half of the Nineteenth Century.

Each of us tried the mountain oysters and some of us—Felicia and Richard—even professed a liking for them. I was just glad I was able to swallow mine without barfing.

Sunday's mule trip down the canyon was an experience of a lifetime. We descended twenty-three hundred feet on the narrow ledges prior to heading back to the top.

At lunch we traded impressions and Jim said, "I couldn't believe how far I would've fallen if my mule tripped. The gorge is so deep it looks like the bottom of the world."

Susan said, "I hear you. Our guides told us no mule has ever slipped over the edge in the park's history but the mule bones I saw below the trail belied his assurance."

"You probably saw the bones of some other animal," Jarrett countered.

Felicia said, "The ride was a little scary for me too but mainly I was awed by the surrounding splendor. I didn't expect to see towering pines and aspens and a blanket of lush greenery in an Arizona desert."

I flew Felicia, Susan, and Richard to Phoenix's Sky Harbor airport in plenty of time for them to board their airliners. And I got Jarrett, Jim, and me back to Tucson rested, refreshed, and ready for the next hearing.

CHAPTER SEVEN

In court on Monday I noticed Kaya Kabotie, Axelrod's boss, sitting at the prosecution table again.

Judge Warren said, "Good morning, everyone. I'll begin by giving the defense the ruling I owe them on their motion for a more diverse jury pool. Mr. Armstrong, although your arguments are novel and persuasive, I don't have the jurisdiction to overrule an entire body of Ninth Circuit law."

"I'm not asking you to, Your Honor. The decisions relying on <u>Duren</u> are academic since our motion is based on the <u>Jones</u> precedent."

"I'll let the circuit court settle the question. The motion is denied."

"Your Honor, <u>Jones</u> is clear and concise. In the interests of conserving judicial resources, I move for you to reconsider. There's a substantial likelihood your denial will be countermanded on appeal, necessitating a costly and time-consuming new trial."

"Motion for reconsideration is denied."

"Exception for the record and I ask you to hear Mr. Hudson on a related matter."

"Mr. Hudson."

Jarrett gave Axelrod and the clerk copies of his brief before he said, "Your Honor, the defense requests you stay the proceedings to allow the Ninth Circuit time to consider an interlocutory appeal of your decision. Appeals prior to a verdict and sentence are disfavored but late last year the Supreme Court upheld their rare necessity. In <u>Mohawk Industries v. Cartwright</u> the justices unanimously ruled that intermediate appeals should be granted in cases involving a constitutional right which would be irreparably lost if review was only available after final judgment. The case at hand conforms to the high Court's standard. Unless Lieutenant Johnson is tried by a fair cross-section of all members of the community he will be deprived of his Sixth Amendment guarantee to an impartial jury, a constitutional infringement no post-conviction appellate panel could undo. Submitted."

"I'll see the defendant and counsels in chambers."

"Looks like we've given the judge cause to pause," Ned said.

"We'll soon find out," I said and Ned, Jarrett, Jim, and I went to the judge's office to find Axelrod, Metcalf, and Kabotie standing by the doorway.

Kabotie and I smiled at each other and she said, "It's good to see you again, David."

"Good to see you too, Kaya. Are you fascinated by preliminary hearings?"

"Not generally. Judge Warren asked me to be here today."

The secretary answered her intercom then told us we could go in.

Judge Warren motioned for us to take chairs, received a nod from the court reporter, and said, "We're on the record. The defendant and all counsels are present. Kaya Kabotie, the manager of the Tucson U.S. Attorney's office, is also in attendance per my request. Although the defense's motion for a more diverse jury pool has some merit, I'm convinced the reliance on the old law of <u>Jones</u> is misplaced and I've ruled per <u>Duren</u> that the motion failed to prove systematic under-representation of a minority group in the county's jury rolls. A case cannot be made that Native Americans are purposefully excluded from Pima County juries."

Warren paused to take a sip of his coffee. "However, an interlocutory appeal will necessitate a long delay in the trial so I'll address the defense's concern another way. The jury commissioner has taken many pro-active steps to increase the participation of Native Americans in the county's judicial system but the response, especially from those living on the county's reservation, continues to be lackluster. The twelve-thousand Native Americans residing in Tucson are more accessible and, taking the suggestions of Mr. Armstrong, and Ms. Kabotie, I'll ask the jury commissioner to subpoena four city-dwelling Native Americans to compel their service in the current federal jury pool. Their addition will bring Native American representation to a percentage sufficient to overcome a statistical challenge under <u>Jones</u>. Of course, since the pool members are randomly selected for *voir dire* questioning there's no guarantee any Native Americans will make the final panel. Still, we now have the chance and, in further pursuit of choosing unbiased jurors, I'll allow counsels to participate in the questioning of the candidates. Each side will have twenty minutes. What are your reactions?"

Kaya said, "My colleagues and I endorse the idea, Your Honor."

"Mr. Armstrong?"

"The defense team does too and we'll forego the interlocutory appeal."

"Noted and appreciated. You all may return to the courtroom. I'll join you shortly."

As we walked to our tables Kaya said, "David, I'm sure the threat of an immediate appeal and a delay of trial was a calculated ploy but you and your associates did pressure a federal judge in this jurisdiction to acknowledge the jury imbalance problem more than any other attorneys ever have."

"What's Mr. Sloan's position in this matter?"

"He hasn't said. He's keeping a low profile. Overcharging Mr. Johnson and indicting him for a non-existent crime will take awhile to live down. As long as we have a few moments let's talk about the possibility of a plea bargain. Should Mr. Johnson be convicted of the second-degree murder charge the minimum guideline sentence would be fourteen years imprisonment. Should Mr. Johnson plead guilty to the charge he'd receive credit for cooperation with the Government and qualify for a sentence as low as eight years, which as a first-offender he'd qualify to serve on probation."

I looked to Ned who said, "I can't admit to something I didn't do just to save my skin, Big Sister. I was justified in killing the Mexican."

Kaya said, "Mr. Johnson's referring to the meaning of my first name in the Hopi language. I'll keep the offer open, David. If he changes his mind, let me know and we can close this case to everyone's satisfaction."

When Judge Warren returned to the bench he said, "I apologize to you media representatives and other spectators for the secrecy. Sometimes negotiations behind closed doors are fruitful. For your information the defense will not file an interlocutory appeal of my denial of their motion for a more racially diverse jury. I'll request the county jury commissioner subpoena enough Native Americans to achieve an even larger percentage in the jury pool than they are in the general population. I'll also allow defense and government lawyers to ask questions of the jury candidates during the selection process. Mr. Armstrong, at next week's hearing I'll expect you to furnish the defense witness list to Mr. Axelrod and the court. Any questions or comments, Counsels?"

"None from the Government," Axelrod said.

"None from the defense," I echoed.

"We're adjourned until next Monday."

I asked Ned and Emily if they had time for coffee with us. They said they did and on our way out I waved goodbye to Kaya and the two prosecutors.

We found an isolated table in the building's cafeteria and I took out a yellow pad. "Ned, we need some people to testify on your behalf. Any ideas you and Emily have are welcome."

Emily said, "The Chairman of the Nation would be good. He's known Ned all his life."

"Please write his name on the pad. Ned, is there a minister or some other religious figure who would speak well of you?"

"Wind Runner, the old medicine man, but I doubt a predominately Christian jury would put much credence in anything he says."

"Don't prejudge at this point. Let's just come up with possible witnesses and we'll cull the list later."

Jim said, "The chief agent of the Tucson Border Patrol spoke highly of Ned as did a DEA supervisor."

Emily said, "Ned and the previous chief of the police department were close. Also Ned and his high school principal."

"What about relatives other than your parents, Ned?" Jim asked.

"There are lots of Johnson's and Garcia's to pick from on the rez."

"Write down the names of those who are or have been leaders in the community."

When Ned was finished Emily said, "David, you need to know Ned was awarded a Distinguished Service Cross and a Purple Heart in the first Gulf War for carrying two members of his platoon to safety after they were cut down by Iraqi snipers. And the previous Tohono O'odham police department chief honored him with a ribbon of valor for pulling a woman and a young girl from a burning car."

"Thanks, Emily. Ned, what's you opinion of FBI Agent Dale Watson?"

"He's a washed out man who hates his lowly job. He treats the Nation's police officers like Mayberry RFD cops but he's such a sloppy investigator himself Chief Rivas never notifies him of a federal crime on the reservation until our detectives and technicians have secured and examined the scene. Last year Watson bungled evidence against a Sioux Indian radical suspected of planting a pipe bomb in a Border Patrol vehicle and a federal judge had to dismiss the case."

"Did Watson handle his interrogation of you by the book?"

"Not by any book I ever read in training. I stopped him from advising me of my Miranda rights by saying I already knew them and he mistakenly accepted my statement as a waiver. We cops also aren't supposed to ask suspects leading questions when we're taking their confessions but Watson tried to trick me into admitting it took too long to drive the Mexican to the desert for me to have acted out of provocation. Truth is, I was still mightily provoked by what he did to my family when I tied him to stakes and left him to die. For all I knew he was already dead. He'd lost a lot of blood from the gunshot wound and wasn't showing any signs of consciousness."

"Thanks for your's and Emily's input on witnesses. Jarrett, Jim, and I will settle on which ones we'll put on the stand and either of you think of any others in the meantime, give me a call."

"We will. I'm grateful to you guys. In no time at all you maneuvered the U.S. Attorney to drop the first-degree murder charge I was facing the death penalty for, browbeat the judge into putting some Indians in the jury pool, and have got me thinking you may win the trial."

Jarrett said, "That is our unmitigated goal, Ned."

"Wouldn't that be a nice ending to the story," Emily said, taking Ned's arm. "Come on, Tonto. Take your pale-faced lover to your wigwam and ravish her."

Ned grinned. "I'd rather put on a mask and play the Lone Ranger for a change. You can be the lonely and unfulfilled school marm only pretending you don't want me to barge into your bedroom."

"Whatever makes your feather quiver, Big Boy."

CHAPTER EIGHT

Tuesday Jim notified us the background checks on the jury pool members and the prosecution's witnesses were done and we used the information Richard emailed us to begin rating the jury candidates on Cheryl's spreadsheet and pinpoint areas of vulnerability of the witnesses.

Dr. Shapiro called me on Wednesday. "David, I've gone over the autopsy of the man your client is accused of murdering. The medical examiner's conclusion that he couldn't determine whether the man died from the gunshot wound or from the attacks by desert creatures is a cop-out. There are many indicators the entrance wound to the man's rib cage was post-mortem. The cause of the man's death was unquestionably the gunshot. The mechanism of death was internal bleeding and hypovolemic shock from the bullet perforating the stomach and the kidney. The manner of death was homicide."

"What is hypovolemic shock?"

"Rapid loss of blood. I would send you my report but you'd have to share it with the prosecution and I'd have to come to Arizona to testify. My family and I'll be at our Nova Scotia summer home in August so I'd prefer you bluff my appearance as you have many times in the past and save me the trip. The day my reputation alone doesn't intimidate a lowly deputy county medical examiner is the day I hang up my lab coat."

"No problem. This is at least the second time this ME made a mistake on a post-mortem wound. A few years back a nineteen-year old girl was raped and killed after a rave party in Tucson. Police discovered a wooden club and a knife at the scene. Fingerprints on the club and the knife matched different suspects but the suspect who'd held the knife was charged with the murder based on the ME's finding that stab wounds caused the girl's death."

"The Amber Hester case?"

"Yes."

"I remember. The defense attorney hired a private pathologist who detected no evidence of blood in the girl's lungs, a conclusive indication she was dead when she was stabbed. You can easily disgrace the ME when he testifies and I'll give you a quick class in death for dummies so you'll know even more reasons why animals didn't kill the Mexican. Grab a pad and pen."

I followed his instructions and soon had two pages filled with notes on forensic topics in both medical jargon and layman language.

"Thanks for your help, Doc. Let Cheryl know how much we owe you and she'll mail you a check."

By Friday Jarrett, Jim, and I finished rating the jury candidates and settled on our witnesses. We would list Dr. Shapiro but not call him. One person we'd actually put on the stand was the company commander who recommended Ned for the Distinguished Service Cross and Purple Heart medals. Jim tracked down the retired Army officer in South Carolina and in return for us paying his expenses he agreed to come to Tucson and testify in the trial. Our other witnesses were the Chairman of the Tohono O'odham Nation; the previous chief of the reservation's police department; the medicine man; and Emily.

We would also inform the judge and the prosecution of our intent to raise a justified homicide defense.

Sunday we accepted Ned's invitation to have dinner with him, Emily, and several of our witnesses at the Desert Diamond Casino near the Tucson airport. The Tohono O'odham Nation owned and operated two other gambling establishments on their land. The casino we were directed to was their newest and glitziest.

We saw a sign in the lobby advertising a performance later in the evening by the Temptations, the Motown group formed in the nineteen-sixty's, and I said I didn't know they were still around.

Jim said, 'You'll hear lots of blasts from the past if you frequent Indian casinos and small city hotel cocktail lounges."

A hostess led us into the Diamond Buffet Room and pointed to a solitary leather banquette on a raised platform, "Lieutenant Johnson and his party aren't here yet but he has the VIP table up there reserved. Make yourselves comfortable."

Ned and Emily soon arrived with Chief Rivas and three other men Ned presented as Frank Saunders, the previous police chief; Wind Runner, the medicine man; and Noah Jordon, Jr., the Chairman of the Tohono O'odham Nation.

They settled around the table and a waitress came to ask if we'd like refreshments.

Ned said, "Order anything you like. Sodas and juices are included in the price of the buffet but thanks to Chief Rivas I'm still on the payroll and can afford to buy stronger drinks for anyone who wants them."

Wind Runner's ancient eyes came to life. "I'll have a double Jim Beam."

"With water and ice?"

"No thanks, Miss. Just a glass of Beam and Beam."

Jarrett, Jim, and I ordered scotches, Ned and Emily chose steins of draft beer, and Rivas, Jordon, and Saunders requested Cokes.

I said I thought alcohol was prohibited on all Indian reservations and Ned responded. "We created wet zones for our casinos. The rest of the rez is still dry."

"Officially," Noah Jordon said. "However, the Three Points Trading Post a few miles off the reservation on the highway to Tucson has the undisputed reputation of selling more beer and booze than any outlet in the area and most of their sales are to our people."

The waitress brought the drinks and Wind Runner looked at Ned. "Don't fret over your budget, Young Wind Runner. We all know the check will be comped in honor of Chairman Noah's presence."

"Why did you call Ned Young Wind Runner, sir?" I asked.

"I was once the fastest runner on the reservation and competitors came from other settlements to challenge me. All of them except Ned failed. The reason most Tohono O'odham think I retired undefeated is Ned never told anyone he beat me. Why is that, Young Wind Runner?"

"It was no one else's business. Why brag? I was decades younger than you and I wasn't sure it actually happened."

Wind Runner grinned in approval. "He was only a kid but I was so impressed with his early wisdom and maturity I took him under my wing and taught him the secret ways of our people. He's even qualified to be a medicine man himself if he ever wants to take that path."

Emily said, "Ned, you told me no one ever bested Wind Runner in a foot race."

"I wasn't lying. My memory is clouded. When I visualize myself ahead of him at the finish line I wonder if I'm drawing on a recollection of reality or a dream, perhaps even a fantasy? I don't know the answer and neither does the one who is the font of all knowledge—the Holy Man himself. He's just playing with your minds."

Emily looked to Wind Runner for a reaction but his expression was inscrutable.

"Let's grab some grub," Ned said and we all followed him to the seafood buffet.

I was about to fill my plate with oysters, shelled shrimp, and Snow Crab legs until I followed the lead of Ned, Emily, Saunders, and Wind Runner and filled a bowl with the Native Salad—a mixture of tepary beans, corn, diced cactus, onions, cucumbers, and chili peppers.

We took our food to the table and Emily said, "What do you think, David?"

"I think your organization's encouragement of Tohono O'odhams to subsist on the traditional crops of the land will improve their spirits as well as their health."

"Jim grew tired of the native food during his short stay on the reservation but you seem content."

"More than content. This salad brings back memories. I grew up on a farm in Arkansas and we grew almost everything we ate. If I remember correctly, the only products we bought in stores were sugar, flour, and a few condiments."

Wind Runner said, "Then you know something of our way of life, David. Mother Earth is our sacred entity and provider of all that is necessary. Emily and others are helping the people on the reservation reclaim their heritage and live in unity with nature. They're also learning they don't need calendars to know when it's time to harvest saguaro fruit, prickly pears, cactus, squash, beans, and other crops. All they have to do is respect and observe the same seasonal patterns our ancestors did for thousands of years. During my eighty-five years in the Nation I've seen many changes but I've seen many more things remain the same."

"How about you, Mr. Saunders?" Jarrett asked. "What will you say to the jurors about Ned?"

"Like Wind Runner, I was impressed with Ned's early maturity. He started hanging around the police department in his early teens and volunteering to help out any way he could. The day after he graduated from high school he applied for a position and I hired him without hesitation. We didn't have a cadet academy so I sent him to the Federal Law Enforcement Training Center in Georgia for five months and got back about the most perfect police officer a chief could ask for. Ned was such a natural leader he made sergeant in a year. And in only his second month on the job he earned a ribbon of valor for the most astonishing example of bravery and strength I've ever seen.

"Late one afternoon a woman and daughter from Tucson were on Highway 86 returning from a tour of the Kitt Peak Observatory when the front wheel of their SUV veered off the pavement. The woman overcorrected, causing the SUV to roll over several times and end up lying on the driver's side.

Luckily, the accident happened less than two miles from Sells so our officers and firefighters were on the scene quickly. By the time I arrived the vehicle's engine was on fire and flames beneath the chassis were heading towards the fuel tank despite the foam retardant the firefighters were spraying. The two occupants were trapped in their seats and crying for help but everyone except Ned was staying back in anticipation of the gas explosion. He opened the upside front door with so much force he almost broke the hinges, badly burning his hand in the process. He then hopped up to the opening and used his knife to puncture the girl's airbag, cut the seat belt harness, and lift her out to safety. He was a nineteen year old kid, his right hand was burned to the bone, he had to douse the flames on his pant's legs but he demanded two fire fighters hold his ankles while he hung down from the opening to free the mother and lift her out of the SUV. She was a good-sized woman weighing between a hundred and forty and a hundred and fifty pounds. How much do you weigh, Ned?"

"One eighty-five."

"How much did you weigh back then?"

"One eighty-five."

"Yet you lifted her out as if she was as light as the young girl and none too soon. You'd barely turned her over to the paramedics when the SUV blew up like a bomb. I saw what you did with my own eyes and I still find it hard to believe."

"People can sometimes call on superhuman strength in dire emergencies," Noah Jordon said. "I read an article awhile back about a mother who raised the rear end of a full-size Chevy sedan that had fallen on her son while he was changing a tire."

Wind Runner said, "Elder Brother possesses all the energy in the universe. All we have to do is tap into his source when necessary."

Emily looked at Jarrett, Jim, and me. "Elder Brother is the Tohono O'odhams Creator."

"Thanks for the explanation," Jim said. "That was an amazing story, Mr. Saunders. Ned was honored for bravery and promoted to sergeant before he was twenty years old. What happened next?"

"I was drafted by the Army," Ned said. "One arm of the federal government has a hard time finding Indian jurors but another arm had no problem locating me and lots of other young men on the rez to use as cannon fodder in Iraq."

Chief Rivas said, "When you returned two years later as a war hero for another act of bravery is where I came in. Frank's diabetes forced him to retire early so I took over the Department and had the good fortune to watch you continue your remarkable career. You made lieutenant by the age of thirty and were cramming for the captain's exam when you were arrested. I hope with every fiber of my being you're acquitted and return to what you do best. I need you. The Nation needs you. Wherever you are is a better place for your being there."

"Thanks, Chief."

Chairman Jordon spoke up for the first time. "Good people come from good stock. Ned's parents were the salt of the earth and so are all his relatives on both sides. There isn't a bad Johnson or Garcia on the reservation. Genes count. The grandfather Ned is named after was a brave and strong man. The story is told of a band of Apache warriors riding through our territory stealing horses and kidnapping women in the old days. In contrast to the fierce and hostile Apaches, our people are generally peaceful so the warriors encountered no resistance until they came upon Mr. Johnson's spread. Hearing his wife's screams, he ran from the field to confront the warriors. One of them jumped off his horse with a lance in hand but Mr. Johnson used a tomahawk to fell him with one fatal blow to the head. He then picked up the man's lance to run through a second warrior and knock yet another out with the tomahawk before the rest retreated. Do you know what he did with the two unconscious warriors they left behind, Ned?"

"I was told he dragged them into the desert, spread-eagled them on stakes, and left them to die."

"You were told right."

Everyone at the table became silent until I said, "Ned's fortunate to have you as friends. Chief Rivas, how can Ned still receive a paycheck if he's suspended from duty?"

"He's on paid administrative leave. I'm treating him the same way I would any officer accused of but not convicted of a crime."

"Is here any policy against him wearing his uniform in court?"

"No."

"Then get your Class A's cleaned and pressed, Ned. From the first day of the trial until the end I want the jurors to see you in uniform."

"Won't that unfairly impress the jurors?" Emily asked.

"All's fair in love in war, and a trial is a war in which words and impressions are the weapons instead of bullets."

"Starting August 9th I'll look like a poster officer for the Department," Ned said and signaled our waitress for the check. She came to the table but, as the all-wise Wind Runner predicted, she informed Ned the casino manager was comping our party's food and drinks in honor of Chairman Jordon's patronage. Jordon nodded in gratitude and Ned left a cash tip on the table.

Jarrett, Jim, and I said goodbye to our client and his witnesses in the parking lot and went back to the Radisson. I was so keyed up from the dinner meeting I endured the heat and sat on my suite's balcony to have a few pipe smokes and drinks before I phoned Felicia at her Belvedere, California home.

"So you've arrived," I said when she answered.

"Yes. I got in late last night and I've taken my time settling in today. The weather is glorious here. Is Tucson still as hot as Hades?"

"Unrelenting. Without air-conditioning I'd be a burnt out shell of myself. But I should be able to join you by the middle of the month. I'll be surprised if the trial lasts more than a week."

"May your estimate come true. I miss my playmate."

"Your playmate misses you too."

CHAPTER NINE

Monday's hearing was attended by more reporters and spectators than we'd seen before, probably due to the increased publicity as the start of the trial neared.

Axelrod and Metcalf were at the prosecution table and Ned and Emily were in their places at our table.

Jarrett, Jim, and I waved at our legal opponents and received a welcoming embraces from Emily. Not the hugging type, Ned gave us fist bumps.

I took copies of our witness list to Axelrod and the court clerk and a few moments later a man came to the rail to address me. "Armstrong, I'm Special Agent Dale Watson. Your investigator has been asking questions about me and I want you to know I'll sue you and him for slander if you besmirch my reputation when I take the stand for the Government."

"You should know anything said in a trial is immune from civil or criminal culpability, Agent Watson."

"There are other ways to get back at you. Do you really want to be on the FBI's secret shit list?"

"Are you recording this conversation on your laptop, Jim?"

"From the beginning."

Watson made an abrupt departure and Ned asked Jim if he really was recording the conversation.

"No and I doubt he really thinks I was but he can't be sure so David's gambit probably stymied him. If not, he's in a world of trouble. A few years and cases ago a couple of Feebies made a similar threat to David and me. Each of them ended up paying a quarter of a million dollars in damages and losing their jobs after we sicced Mel Berger on them."

The bailiff called for order as Judge Warren came in. "Counsels, the jury commissioner was successful in adding four Native Americans to our jury pool—a Navajo, a Pascua Yaqui, an Apache, and a Tohono O'odham. My clerk has copies of the questionnaires for you to pick up when you leave. Mr. Armstrong, are you ready to reveal the witnesses for the defense?"

"Yes, Your Honor. I delivered our list to the prosecution and your clerk before the session began. We will call Talton Long, a retired U.S. Army colonel; Emily Crenshaw, Lieutenant Johnson's fiancé; Wind Runner, a Tohono O'odham Nation medicine man; Frank Saunders, a former chief of the Nation's police department; Noah Jordon, Jr., the Nation's chairman; and Dr. Philip Shapiro, an independent forensic pathologist. We haven't taken written statements from any of our witnesses but other than Dr. Shapiro the testimony of all of them will relate to Lieutenant Johnson's good character. We'll end our case by having Lieutenant Johnson testify in his own behalf and establish grounds for the affirmative defense of justified homicide."

Axelrod said, "Your Honor, it would be in keeping with the spirit of reciprocal discovery if Mr. Armstrong would tell us the purpose of his forensic expert's appearance."

"I'll be glad to, Your Honor. Dr. Shapiro will refute the county medical examiner's findings from A to Z."

Warren allowed himself a hint of a grin. "Maybe not the answer you wanted, Mr. Axelrod—an answer nevertheless. Mr. Armstrong, what is Wind Runner's legal name?"

"Luis Rios but he's called Wind Runner by almost everyone on the reservation."

"Does either side have any motions to make today?"

Neither Axelrod nor I did and the judge adjourned court for a week.

Jim picked up our copies of the four questionnaires from the clerk then we went to the building cafeteria with Ned and Emily to talk about the new jury candidates.

After we brought cups of coffees to the table Jim looked through the questionnaires and said, "Here's who we've got. Monica Tapahonso is a Navajo living in Tucson and employed by the county as a social worker. She's thirty-eight, divorced, and has a twelve-year old daughter who lives with relatives on the reservation near Phoenix. Florence Benally is a Pascua Yaqui. She's twenty, single, and attending Pima Community College. Kelwyn Kapook is a thirty year old, single, Apache set designer for the Arizona Theatre Company. And Luz Pablo is a forty-four year old, married, Tohono O'odham nurse at the reservation's Healing Rain House Medical Clinic. Do you know her or her husband, Ned?"

"No. The clinic is in San Xavier, a small settlement on the northwest corner of the reservation fifty miles from the area I work. You were there on Saturday night when we met at the Desert Diamond Casino. The three women sound OK to me but we can't have the Apache guy on the jury. The words for enemy and Apache are the same in our language. There's too big a chance the ancient enmity between our Nations will bias him against me."

"I see your point but I'll need a solid reason for dismissing him. Lawyers are no longer able to peremptorily challenge a member of a minority without proving the challenge isn't racially based. The problem may not surface, though. There's only a one in a hundred and four chance he'll be randomly selected for questioning."

Jarrett asked if the clinic the Tohono O'odham nurse worked for was government operated and Emily said, "Yes. Healing Rain House is run by the Indian Health Service."

We finished our coffees, said farewell to Ned and Emily, and left the courthouse.

Jarrett, Jim, and I returned to the hotel and lounged by the pool the rest of the day.

We subsisted on bar snacks for lunch, caught up on phone calls, and checked in with our respective offices.

Cheryl, Will, Burt, and Arthur told me all was well at the Project.

And when I talked to Felicia in the late afternoon she told me her vacation was being interrupted by calls from lobbyists for Bay Area businesses. "They seem to think the Supreme Court ruling granting corporations as much right as individuals to lobby for political influence entitles them to receive specific favors in return for their contributions. I have to remind the lobbyists that bribery is still illegal.'"

"Aren't tawdry exchanges of money rare."

"Money is only one of the temptations legislators face. My first major achievement as a newbie in the Senate was passing a bill establishing thousands of acres of Northern California coastline as a National Recreational Area. What you and most people don't know is the legislation would've never been enacted if I hadn't yielded to the demand of the then Chairwoman of the powerful Appropriations Committee to grandfather in lucrative mineral rights to a company controlled by her husband. I thought she was the personification of Lucifer and considered myself a manipulated victim. Since then I've come to realize how easily we succumb to the need to retain power and forgiven my misdeed. Will you also forgive me?"

"Nisha, we're all a history of good and bad acts and we all harbor secrets we're hesitant to expose to others. The beans you just spilled to me don't change my opinion of you in the least. I still consider you one the most ethical people in my life."

"Sounds like you love me despite my faults."

"Isn't that the definition of unconditional love?"

"Yes and I love you unconditionally too, my always dependable hunk. Have a nice night and we'll talk again tomorrow."

Drenched in sweat from the oppressive heat, I dove into the pool and luxuriated in the relatively cool water, thinking I would choose to live almost anywhere other than a desert.

I went back to my suite in time to shower, change clothes, and host the cocktail hour.

Jarrett raised his glass of scotch. "Here's to the far-reaching and virtually limitless resources of the internet. Down at the pool I was researching suppression motions on my laptop and came across a recent Supreme Court case I'm pretty sure we can use to get Ned's confessions thrown out. The case was like a diamond in a field of rocks waiting to be discovered. Have either of you heard of Corley v. U.S.?"

Jim and I shook our heads and Jarrett said, "By a seven to two majority—only the Neanderthal reactionary justices Antonini and Clarendon dissenting—the Court held that a person suspected of committing a federal crime must be presented to a magistrate within six hours of arrest or all information obtained during interrogation is inadmissible evidence. In Corley the information obtained was a voluntary confession."

"Holy Cow," I exclaimed. "You found a bombshell to blow the enemy out of the water. Ned wasn't taken to a magistrate until the day after his arrest."

"Please access and read the decision on your laptop now. Jim read it by the pool."

I did as Jarrett asked then told him his assessment of Corley was correct.

Jim said, "While our appellate whiz was discovering the legal tactics equivalent of the theory of relativity I ran background checks on the four Indian jury pool members. The Navajo and the Tohono O'odham women have spotless records but the Pasca Yaqui college student has been arrested twice for possession of pot. The charges were dropped each time when she completed drug diversion programs. And the Apache is a member of AIM, an organization of militant American Indians."

I said, "If Axelrod is privy to the same information, he may want to keep the Apache off the jury as much as we do. Drive the Land Rover out to see Ned and Rivas tomorrow and let them know what we're up to. I'm expect Ned will approve but Rivas may have a conflict with doing anything to upset the

FBI. If not, take his affidavit about how long Ned was held in the reservation jail until Watson came for him."

Jarrett splashed more scotch in our glasses and I continued. "The very real possibility of Ned's confessions being suppressed has me excited and thinking we should consider an all or nothing strategy by telling the judge we don't want the jurors to have the option of convicting him of voluntary manslaughter if they acquit him of second-degree murder."

Jim said, "Are you hoping to prevent the jury from reaching a compromise verdict?"

"Precisely. Whenever possible I like to keep things simple for them. To paraphrase H.L. Mencken, no one ever lost a trial by underestimating the intelligence of American jurors."

"Cynical yet oh so true," Jarrett said. "I endorse the all or nothing approach, David. In my opinion the mandated instructions to jurors on homicide are fair regarding murder but they almost force a manslaughter conviction."

Jim said, "Plus the strategy will give us the best chance of sending Ned home a free man. If he agrees, I say we put all our chips in the pot and roll the dice. I'll let you know what Ned thinks when I talk to him tomorrow."

"Good. I'm getting hungry. Unless either of you have a better idea I'd like to go back to the casino for some more native food. They'll obviously have entrees you two will want to eat too."

They were amenable and we made the short trip to the casino while we could still see San Xavier in daylight.

I was struck by the difference between the community and the ones Chief Rivas showed me in another part of the reservation. San Xavier wasn't as isolated as those settlements, the housing was more modern, and there were many more new vehicles in evidence.

Jarrett theorized the San Xavier residents were profiting from the Desert Diamond Casino. Jim demurred, saying Ned told him revenues from the reservation's three casinos were distributed evenly to every member of the Tohono O'odham Nation.

It was American Night in the casino's buffet room, which was fine with Jarrett and Jim. Me too when I saw tepary beans were one of the side dishes. I piled a helping of them onto a large oval plate along with a pork chop, mashed potatoes, corn on the cob, squash, sliced tomatoes and onions, and biscuits and I was back in Pickles Gap, Arkansas for the moment.

CHAPTER TEN

Jim went to Sells on Tuesday morning to see Ned and Chief Rivas and I didn't hear from him until past eight in the evening when Jarrett and I were dining on Chinese food in my suite.

"Save me some," he said. "I'll be there soon."

When he arrived he ate the remaining portions of every take-out container on the table, belched, took a swig of scotch, and said, "Ned is fully supportive of the motion to suppress his confessions. So is Rivas. Having to refer all the reservation's serious felonies to the FBI irks the chief as does the legislation requiring the procedure. He says the Major Crimes Act passed by Congress in 1885 under the theory Indians weren't competent to deal with complicated cases was racist but the law is still enforced. Speaking of racism, the reason I've been gone so long is Rivas was tied up most of the day giving the Mexican-hating Arizona Governor and several aides a tour of the reservation and the border."

I said, "So when Rivas was finally free you and he went into his old trailer behind police headquarters and crafted his affidavit around a bottle of Dewar's White Label?"

"You're a discerning man. You can read the affidavit later. For now I'll give you a summary." Glancing at his notebook, Jim continued. "The day of the murders Ned got to Rivas's office at one-thirty in the afternoon to tell him what happened. Rivas notified the Special Agent in charge of the FBI's Tucson office, sent tribal cops to protect the two crime scenes, and asked the county medical examiner's office to send out a pathologist. Agent Watson phoned Rivas to say he was waiting to testify in a trial in Tucson and would come to Sells as soon as he could to pick up Ned. Rivas put Ned in a holding cell but left the door ajar for Emily to come and go and bring him meals from the Desert Rain Café. Watson appeared at eleven thirty-five the next morning and asked Rivas to show him the crime scenes. They returned in the early afternoon and Watson took Ned into custody.

"The rest of the time-line comes from Watson's report. He transported Ned to the Agency's offices in Tucson, interrogated him from two-fifteen to three-twenty, videotaped his confession, wrote up a complaint, and finally presented him to a magistrate at four-thirty, twenty-seven hours after Ned turned himself into Rivas. From my reading of <u>Corley</u>, the suppression motion is a slam-dunk."

"From my reading too," I said. "Jarrett, file the motion along with a request for an evidentiary hearing. You'll argue the brief and conduct the hearing."

"I'll subpoena Watson and ask Rivas to voluntarily attend. Should I also file motions for the Miranda violation and the lack of a warrant to seize blood samples from Ned's boots?"

"Compose them as back-ups to be filed only if Warren denies the more encompassing motion to suppress the confessions. Jim, what did Ned think of our idea of going for an acquittal by not giving jurors the option of convicting him of voluntary manslaughter?"

"He gave us *carte blanche* to do what we think is best. What he told me was touching. I laid out the tactic we were considering and explained the pros and cons and he told me the most frightened he'd ever been was during an initiation rite. Wind Runner took him to the base of Baboquivari Peak where their God, Elder Brother, lives. Only medicine men like Wind Runner know the way through the maze to Elder Brother's home and Ned said he followed Wind Runner through dark, narrow passageways until he saw in a bright flash of light his life as it had been, as it might've been, and as it could be in the future. He came out of the maze a changed man no longer afraid to be led anywhere by Wind Runner and he told me he felt the same way about you, Jarrett, and me. He trusts us to lead him safely through the legal maze."

"Hot damn. Now we can launch a full-fledged attack on the Government's case on Monday."

Jarrett grinned. "You really get off on trials, don't you?"

"For sure. I cherish my relationship with Felicia. I derive satisfaction from the companionship and give and take of friends and co-workers. I also love to eat good food, fly planes, and sail boats but nothing pumps me up like fighting for a client in court."

"It shows."

The court clerk called on Thursday to inform me Judge Warren felt the supporting papers filed with the suppression motion provided him sufficient information. An evidentiary hearing wouldn't be necessary.

Jarrett said, "I'll let Agent Watson and Chief Rivas know they no longer have to appear. Warren must've decided to suppress the confessions. He couldn't possibly be thinking of summarily denying the motion without a hearing."

We heard a different slant on Sunday when we met Charlie Nelson and Drew Patterson at McMahon's Steak House again and Drew said, "David, your request for the judge to throw out Ned Johnson's confessions is causing havoc in his chambers and in the U.S. Attorney's office downtown. The word is nobody from either branch of the Government can find any case law to dispute the motion so the judge may defer to the Ninth Circuit for a ruling."

"That would be a cowardly avoidance of responsibility."

"Federal judges are usually not pillars of strength. With few exceptions, the ones I've tried cases before are into self-preservation more than issuing the right decisions."

Charlie said, "You shouldn't have written such a brilliant brief, David. You didn't leave Warren any wiggle room."

"I didn't write the brief. Blame the appellate genius, Jarrett. He's the author and he did the defense proud. Is the U.S. Attorney involved in the havoc over the motion?"

"No. He's been at the Justice Department in Washington trying to save his job, which, according to rumors, is Kaya Kabotie's for the taking. How she handles this broadside by the defense may change the situation, though. Losing the motion would be a real blow to the prosecution's case."

"How do the Indian pool members look?" asked Drew.

Jim said, "Like any four other jury candidates. Two are iffy and two are so-so."

I said, "No matter. We'll still win the trial."

Charlie smiled at my boast. "The Tucson legal establishment has never seen such combative and resourceful criminal attorneys. Most of the ones who practice here are intimidated by federal proceedings."

"Most of the ones who practice in any jurisdiction are intimidated by the feds. That's why an ace like Benjamin Brafman rarely loses a federal case, even though he specializes in defending known members of New York crime families. The judges and prosecutors aren't accustomed to a lawyer who disdains plea bargaining and defends the charges against his clients the old-fashioned way—by forcing the Government to prove each and every element of alleged crimes beyond a reasonable doubt."

"I've heard Brafman's good but you're at the acme of your courtroom skills and you're backed by similarly skilled teammates. If Uncle Sam is ever looking to throw me in the slammer, I'm calling 1-800-David, Jarrett, and Jim."

After dinner Jarrett thanked Charlie and Drew for their tip and said as soon as we were back in our hotel he'd bone up on the law and be prepared to embarrass the judge if he tried to waffle out of a decision on our motion.

The weather was hot with no cloud cover all week and Monday was no different. Our rental car was scorching in the hotel's open parking lot, requiring me to turn on the engine and run the air-conditioner for several minutes before I could touch the wheel and drive us to the federal courthouse.

In Judge Warren's courtroom I noticed Agent Watson on the bench behind the prosecution table wearing a wrinkled suit and a disgruntled expression.

Axelrod and Metcalf didn't appear to be much happier but they still exchanged polite greetings with us.

Emily and Charlie Wilson were on the first bench on the defense side of the room and Ned was at our table.

"You three look like you're on a major adrenalin rush," Ned observed. "If you were officers going on patrol with me, I'd make sure your weapons were on safety."

I laughed. "Don't worry. We won't accidentally shoot you in the back. We're just excited today finally got here and we can raise a legal ruckus. Hello, Charlie. Don't you conduct faculty meetings on Monday mornings?"

"The law school recessed for the summer so I was able to come here."

"We're honored by your presence and looking forward to your input."

The bailiff commanded everyone to stand and Judge Warren made his entrance.

Looking as discomfited as the prosecutors and the FBI agent did, he said, "The court is in receipt of a suppression motion from the defense. I'll hear argument from them first."

Jarrett stepped up to the lectern. "Your Honor, <u>Corley v. U.S.</u>, the recent Supreme Court opinion we cited in our brief, is the only authority you need to suppress the confessions Lieutenant Johnson made during twenty-seven hours of post-arrest detention. <u>Corley's</u> straightforward and un-ambiguous decision compels suppression of all confessions obtained by officers when a suspect is not presented to a magistrate within six hours of arrest. We urge you to decide in Lieutenant Johnson's favor."

"Mr. Axelrod."

"The opinion altered or overturned several precedents so we're unable to offer any cases in rebuttal. However, the justices didn't say they were countermanding Federal Rule of Evidence 700, which holds that all evidence is admissible subject to relevancy and the trial judge's discretion, and we can't believe they intended to abolish such a long-standing statutory authority."

"I agree. The defendant admissions are extremely relevant evidence I'm reluctant to exclude. However, since Corley has far-reaching implications I'll defer the decision to the Ninth Circuit Court of Appeals."

Jarrett said, "Your Honor, the relevancy of confessions isn't a determining factor of their admissibility under Corley. I'll read from page four, paragraph seven of the opinion: 'Federal agents cannot be free to question suspects for extended periods before bringing them out in the open. Custodial interrogations, by their very nature, isolate and pressure individuals to confess to crimes they never committed. Our unequivocal holding that suspects must be presented to a magistrate within six hours of arrest establishes a bright line of law for district court judges to follow to ensure this unconstitutional practice is curtailed once and for all.' End quote. Deferring to the Ninth Circuit would be a waste of judicial resources and contemptuous of the Supreme Court's clear guidelines for lower court judges to follow in Corley situations."

Given no way out of his predicament by Jarrett, the judge still visibly agonized over his decision until, spitting the words out as if they distasteful, finally said, "The motion is granted."

Ned squeezed my knee but didn't otherwise react.

Axelrod said, "Your Honor, the inadmissibility of the confessions has rendered Agent Watson's testimony irrelevant. We remove him from our witness list."

Watson's mumbled protest was silenced by Judge Warren's gavel. "I don't tolerate outbursts from spectators. Mr. Armstrong, does the defense have any other business for the court?"

"We do. We exercise our prerogative to not have the jurors instructed on the lesser included offense of voluntary manslaughter. The well-settled precedent of the Supreme Court in Spaziano v. Florida established this privilege. I'll read from page forty-two of the decision: 'The practice of instructing on lesser-included crimes developed as an aid to the State. If prosecutors failed to present sufficient evidence to prove the predicate crime, they might still persuade the jury the defendant was guilty of something else. We therefore find defendants have a due process right to be tried on only one charge.' End of passage."

Axelrod had no grounds to object and the judge asked Ned to rise.

"Mr. Johnson, have your attorneys told you what they're proposing is considered very risky?"

"Yes, sir."

"Have they explained you're forfeiting an opportunity to be convicted of a much less serious crime than second-degree murder and of being sentenced to a much shorter prison term?"

"Yes, sir."

"And is it still your desire for them to proceed with this line of defense?"

"Yes, sir."

"You may sit. Counsels, the <u>Spaziano</u> case affords me no discretion in this issue. I will accede to the defense's request and not instruct the jurors on voluntary manslaughter. Mr. Axelrod, does the Government have any further discovery obligation to the defense?"

"No, sir."

"Mr. Armstrong, does the defense have any further discovery obligation to the Government?"

"No, Your Honor."

"Then we're adjourned until next Monday when the trial will begin."

As everyone in our small group congratulated Jarrett on winning the suppression motion Charlie said, "Your balanced approach of respect and authoritative reasoning compelled the judge to act when his obvious inclination was to pass the buck. And David, your bold go for broke strategy of not giving jurors the chance to convict Ned of voluntary manslaughter set the prosecutor on his heels. I'm glad a few student interns from the Project office were in the gallery to watch you two perform. Jim, I understand your work is behind the scenes but I'm sure it is just as valuable."

I asked Charlie if we would see him in court next week and he said, "For certain and for every session thereafter."

He excused himself to talk to the interns, and Ned, Emily, Jarrett, Jim, and I left.

Ned was so stimulated by things going our way in the hearing his fist bumps were more energetic than usual.

Before we parted I reminded him to wear his uniform on Monday.

CHAPTER ELEVEN

While Jarrett, Jim, and I were having drinks in my suite late in the afternoon I told Jarrett he could choose any restaurant he wanted for our dinner in honor of his sterling achievement in court.

"Just don't make it Emily's Desert Star Café in Sells," Jim chided.

"Let's try Janos in the Westin Hotel. Sunday's *Daily Star* ran a piece on the most expensive restaurants in Tucson and the reviewer gave Janos the most dollar signs. Here's the phone number."

"Janos it is," I said.

I called the number and requested a table for three at seven o'clock.

"Yes," I said to the person I was talking to. "My boyfriend will be proposing to me."

"What was that about?" Jim asked.

"The woman taking our reservation wanted to know if I was celebrating a special occasion."

Jim howled with laughter and pointed to Jarrett. "You're the boyfriend. Adding race to the gay connection will test the restaurant staff's political correctness to the hilt."

Janos was an up-scale Southwestern restaurant with pastel-colored walls. Our waiter didn't offer a birthday congratulation or treat us any differently than he would've otherwise.

For drinks he recommended a concoction the bar was featuring but we chose classic martinis. They were brought to us in crystal stemware and the waiter asked if we had any questions about the menu.

"Yes," Jim said. "The ten-hour braised short ribs option is tickling my palate but I'm turned off by the Anasazi beans and the yucky fries they come with."

"They're Yucca fries, sir. Our chef incorporates indigenous foods of the area whenever possible but we offer substitutions. Would you prefer creamy mashed potatoes and braised red cabbage?"

"Would I ever."

Jarrett preferred those substitutions too but I asked for the plate as advertised and ordered a bottle of Chateauneuf-du-Pape for the table.

Our selections were served. The long-simmered meat was savory as was the zesty horseradish sauce. I liked the Anasazi beans but the Yucca fries didn't work for me, and Jarrett kindly shared some of his mashed potatoes.

We ended our dining experience drinking the last of the wine on the patio while listening to a jazz combo.

Jarrett said, "How much did the most expensive restaurant in Tucson set you back, David?"

"I haven't seen the check yet. The short ribs were thirty-two bucks a pop, the wine was a hundred and a half, and the three martinis will add at least another thirty so we're probably talking two-hundred and fifty dollars with tip. A modest sum for you finagling a cautious federal judge into acting like a giant of the judiciary."

"Oliver Wendell Holmes he's not but he followed a law he didn't like today and gained a measure of respect from me."

"From me too," Jim said.

I said, "I'm reminded of the federal judge in Manhattan who refused to admit evidence obtained by torture of a suspected terrorist in a secret overseas jail run by the CIA. The Government lawyers pleaded for the judge to change his decision, saying they would have to dismiss the case if he didn't allow the evidence. I'll quote his answer as best I remember: 'The Constitution is the rock upon which our nation rests. We must follow the revered document not only when it is convenient but when its dictates prevent the conviction of a presumably dangerous defendant. To do less would diminish us and undermine the foundation upon which we stand.'"

As soon as I was in my suite again I called Felicia and she asked if I wanted to spend the weekend in her Belvedere digs.

"I would if we weren't picking jurors on Monday. I'll be preoccupied with assessing the candidates' qualifications until then. However, I don't expect the trial to be lengthy and I promise to come see you right after we have a verdict."

"Don't rush justice but don't tarry either. Your woman has needs."

"Which your man will satisfy as soon as he possibly can."

I tuned into a local TV station's late newscast that evening to find out what the weather forecast was and saw a reporter's interview with U.S. Attorney Thomas Sloan in a terminal at the Tucson airport.

> "Mr. Sloan, what is your reaction to the hearing in the Ned Johnson murder case this morning?"

> "I've been in meetings at the Justice Department in D.C. for a few days and have only heard second-hand reports but I'm appalled by Judge Warren's action. Letting a bunch of out of State defense lawyers bamboozle him to issue a ruling that gutted our case is unconscionable. I won't say anymore now. I'm anxious to get home."

> The anchorperson asked the reporter if he was surprised by Sloan's comments and the reporter said, "Very. It's virtually unheard of for a U.S. Attorney to publicly criticize a federal judge. He's clearly frustrated but I can't imagine him escaping a severe reprimand for such a flagrant indiscretion."

I concluded Sloan was having a nervous breakdown and turned off the TV.

Following breakfast with Jarrett and Jim on Tuesday I received a call from Cheryl. "Good morning, David. Have you seen today's *New York Times*?"
"No."
"Pick one up or read the online edition. Cindy Hill has written another ode of adulation about you?"
"Thanks. Say hello to Burt, Arthur, and Will for me."
"When they get back. They've gone to Oxford, Mississippi to hold a press conference with our local manager and our latest released prisoner."
"Darnell Lipscomb. He was on death row for twenty-eight years until one of the Ole Miss student interns found out the Tupelo police still possessed blood evidence from the crime scene. She and two lawyers in the Project's on-campus office got a federal judge to order DNA testing of the blood and Darnell was exonerated. Unfortunately, Mississippi doesn't compensate persons who were wrongfully convicted and when I put a hundred dollars in Darnell's commissary account during my last visit with him he told me he didn't have five cents of his own money and no living relatives."
"I'm sure Burt and Arthur will help him get on his feet. They're as generous as you are, you big sap. In Cindy's piece she says you're terrorizing the judge and prosecutor in Tucson with your aggressive legal maneuvers. Keep up the good work. Other lawyers don't turn your name around and call you Strongarm for nothing."

Cindy Hill, a legal correspondent for the *Times*, was a chronicler of my career and I went online to read her latest chapter. Beneath a photograph of me coming down the steps of the Supreme Court was a headline:

DAVID ARMSTRONG, THE HIGH-PROFILE ATTORNEY DEFENDING AN AMERICAN INDIAN ACCUSED OF MURDERING A MEXICAN DRUG SMUGGLER IS LIVING UP TO HIS REPUTATION FOR COURTROOM THEATRICS.

When Ned Johnson, a tribal police officer on the Tohono O'odham Indian reservation near Tucson, Arizona, was indicted for shooting and leaving to die in the desert a Mexican drug trafficker responsible for the deaths of Johnson's parents and the rape and death of his fifteen-year old sister, his conviction appeared certain.

But then David Armstrong, one of America's most successful trial lawyers and Executive Director of the Innocent Prisoner's Project in New York, agreed to represent Johnson. Now the Arizona U.S. Attorney's case is in shambles.

Armstrong and two associates first forced the prosecution to drop the first-degree murder-torture allegation because no such federal crime exists. And since the reduced charge of second-degree murder doesn't carry a potential death sentence they prevailed on the judge to release Johnson from pre-trial detention. The Armstrong legal team also persuaded the judge to add Indians to the jury pool; throw out Johnson's confessions; and not allow jurors to deliberate on voluntary manslaughter if they acquit Johnson of second-degree murder, which is leading some courtroom observers to think Johnson may not be convicted of any crime.

In his nearly two decade career Armstrong has lost only one trial—the case of a priest who killed a parishioner during an exorcism—and won many sensational ones such as the memorable retrial of Charles Manson. He has the ability to dominate a court with his six-foot two frame, dramatic flair, encyclopedic knowledge of the law, thorough preparation, and winning ways. He was elected as this year's honorary President of the American Criminal Trial Lawyers Association by the largest majority of members in history and the full-time manager of the association says that was because Armstrong has no peers. "David is in a class of one," the manager told me.

Despite flying his own jet, driving expensive sports cars, living on a luxurious yacht in Long Island, and maintaining a long-term relationship with the glamorous U.S. Senator Felicia Bates-Baxter, Armstrong maintains a low profile. He doesn't flaunt his achievements and is notoriously averse to speaking with reporters.

He once explained his reticence to publicity by saying: "Trials are never about me. They're only about my clients so why should I run my mouth in public and risk jeopardizing their chances in court." I didn't have a good answer then and I don't now but I still wish we had a better understanding of what makes this remarkable man tick.

Cindy's number was on my cell phone contact list and I called her. "Thanks for the unsolicited PR. Were you at yesterday's hearing?"

"No. A stringer fed me the details but I'll be there for jury selection on Monday and thereafter. Will you reciprocate for the PR by rating your chances of winning an acquittal for Johnson?"

"What are my two favorite words for media representatives?"

"No comment."

"You get ten points for memory, another point for persistence, and nothing else. See you in court, Scribe."

I braved the heat and went out on my balcony to smoke a pipe and think of questions to ask jury candidates during *voir dire*. I made note of the usual predispositions I needed to expose—dislike of lawyers, presumption of the defendant's guilt, belief in the Government's infallibility, and misunderstanding of the terms burden of proof and reasonable doubt then added prejudice against Indians in general and Tohono O'odham Indians in particular.

Jarrett and Jim came to the suite to say they'd like to take a break and visit Tombstone.

"Is that the reason you're wearing your cowboy costume again?" I asked Jim.

"You got it, Pard."

"I'm too engrossed in trial planning to join you two. Here are the car keys. Take as long as you like, even have dinner there if you like."

"Maybe," Jarrett said. "MapQuest indicates the drive is only a little more than an hour each way. If we're not back by seven, eat without us."

I was in the suite going over all the prosecution's evidence for the umpteenth time when Kaya Kabotie called my cell phone and asked if I was free to meet with her in the Radisson's coffee shop. "I can be there in fifteen minutes."

"Come on by. I'll be wearing a tee-shirt with A PALAPA IN TOPALITO IS BETTER THAN A CONDO IN REDONDO slogan."

"How could I miss you?"

I was already seated at a table in the coffee shop when Kaya came in.

We both asked for cups of tea then she said, "David, I'm sorry to have to move up our post-trial get together but I've been summoned to Washington by the AG and I expect him to ask me to take Thomas Sloan's job."

"That would be quite a step up in your career."

"And quite a problem perhaps. I'm burned out on Justice Department office politics so before I talk to the AG I'd like to know if there's any possibility of working for the Innocent Prisoner's Project. As I mentioned the morning we met, I have great admiration for the organization and would be honored to represent the Project in any way I could."

"And we'd be honored to have you represent us, Kaya. We currently have no openings for managers but we do need a seasoned and reputable attorney like yourself to argue our causes in Arizona, New Mexico, Colorado, and Utah appellate courts, and, when necessary, to federal circuit panels and the U.S. Supreme Court. The salary and benefits are generous and you could set up and staff an office anywhere you desired in the four-state area."

"What a wonderful prospect. My family could move to Flagstaff instead of Phoenix and be right next door to the reservation where so many of our relatives live. How do I apply for the position?"

"You just did and you applied to the ultimate decision maker. I won't hire anyone else until you give me a firm no."

"Don't you have to answer to a board of directors?"

"Only for my results, not my decisions."

"Oh, David, you've made my day. I'll switch hats now and talk to you about Ned Johnson's case. In my capacity as the acting U.S. Attorney for this district I have a new plea bargain offer—voluntary manslaughter with a recommended sentence of probation. I won't insult your intelligence by pretending I'm not grateful for the kindness you've shown me. Please don't insult my character by thinking your kindness has influenced me to lower the charge to a trifle."

"Of course not. I'm sure Ned will turn down the offer anyway. He's not interested in pleading to any crime that will preclude his continued employment as a police officer."

"Then his fate will lie with a jury. You've already put up an amazing defense.

Maybe you'll convince twelve civic-minded people to totally absolve Johnson of criminal responsibility for killing the man who murdered his family."

"I'll try with every fiber of my being."

"I know you will." She looked at my tee-shirt. "Where is Topalito?"

"Fifteen miles north of Puerto Vallarta, Mexico. It's a small village by the sea frozen in time. Why are you acting in Sloan's stead? Has he checked into a loony bin?"

"No, though perhaps he should. I guess it's all right to tell you. The news is certain to come out soon. He was fired. When he went to his office this morning U.S. Marshals were waiting for him. They allowed him to remove his personal belongings under their observation then escorted him from the building."

"Brutal."

"Yes, which is why I'm not sure I want to continue associating with people who are so cold. But Mr. Sloan was the cause of his own downfall. He's one of the most self-centered persons I've ever known. Members of agrarian Indian tribes like the Hopi, Navajo, Pima, and Tohono O'odham are group-oriented. The 'we' pronoun is almost exclusively used. We rarely say 'I' and Mr. Ryan reminded me of something my father said about a chief who took himself too seriously. He told me people who are wrapped up in themselves make very small packages. I'd better go, David. I'm taking a four p.m. flight to Washington and I still have to clear my desk. Thanks for taking the time to see me and thanks for the opportunity we discussed. I'll let you know my decision soon."

Jarrett and Jim got back from Tombstone at half past six and Jim said, "The place is as touristy as Fisherman's Wharf in San Francisco and, like the Wharf, barely worth a one-time visit. We saw the OK Corral, Boot Hill, and had spicy chicken wings and cheese fries at the Central Palace Saloon, one of the first establishments in the original town. Marshal Earp's office was on the second floor next to the Painted Lady's rooms."

"Were you also unimpressed with Tombstone, Jarrett?"

"Pretty much. I would've left right after lunch but Jim wanted to see the last simulated gunfighter duel of the day."

"Did the guy in the white hat win?"

"As always. The owner of the Central Palace Saloon did debunk one Old West myth for us, though. She says the women who milked saloon patrons for drinks, the ones Jim referred to as Painted Ladies, weren't prostitutes. They dressed seductively and danced and sang for the drunken cowboys but at closing time they let them know sex was only available in the brothels off the main street."

"Where they had to wait until Marshal Earp was finished?"

"No. He was with Miss Kitty."

"You're confusing him with Marshal Dillon."

I got obligatory titters from Jarrett and Jim then briefed them on my conversation with Kaya.

"She's sharp," Jarrett said. "If she turns down the promotion and doesn't take the Project job you offered her, let me know. We could use an attorney of her caliber in the firm."

Jim said, "Enough chit chat. What's for supper?"

"How does seafood sound? I took a mid-afternoon pipe smoking stroll and stopped in the Trident Grill a few blocks from here to have a beer. The shellfish plates they were serving looked appetizing and they have an extensive selection of microbrews on tap."

I received two thumbs up and we walked to the Trident. The crowd was mostly a mix of sports fans and University of Arizona college students. A Phoenix Diamondbacks and Washington Nationals baseball game was on a wall-screen TV.

We found an empty table and ordered three pints of Moose Drool ale and a large bucket of peel and eat shrimp.

During our meal a young woman at a table next to ours was frantically trying to repulse the advances of an unruly guy she called Brad.

Jim addressed her. "Is Brad with you?"

"No way. We're acquainted but he sat down without my asking and is acting like I'm his for the taking."

Jim stood up. "Then you'd best leave the lady alone."

"Butt out, Motherfucker," Brad said and stood up himself. He was at least a head taller than Jim and his muscular biceps were bulging against the sleeves of his tee-shirt.

Unimpressed, Jim said, "Leave now. I won't ask again."

"You're cruising for a bruising, old fellow. I'm a former Navy Seal."

"And I'm a former LAPD cop. If you don't disappear in ten seconds, I'll step on your toes."

Brad was wearing flip-flops and Jim was in his cowboy boots but Brad didn't take Jim's threat seriously. "Step on my toes?"

"Five, four, three, two, one and you've missed your deadline," Jim said and ground the heel of his boot into one of Brad's feet.

The no longer quite so tough former Navy Seal cried out and collapsed in a chair wincing in pain.

A member of the staff, presumably a supervisor, rushed to the scene and asked Jim to leave. "I don't care which one of you was in the right. Just leave."

I took some bills out of my pocket to cover the check and the staff member said, "Whatever you had is on the house. Please get out of here of before Brad's buddies show up and cause a riot."

We yielded to the request and on the saunter to the hotel Jim said, "Navy

Seals and members of other elite special forces units are taught how to kill. Cops are taught how to subdue hostile suspects. Big Bad Brad learned one of our simplest tricks tonight. Having your foot stomped on hurts like hell and takes the fight right out of you. So does a punch on the nose. I might've let him slide for bothering the girl but I had to make him pay for calling me an old fellow."

"He may win by losing. The girl was consoling him when we left."

"Women!" Jim exclaimed.

"Humans!" I corrected.

CHAPTER TWELVE

We worked in our separate suites again on Wednesday then convened in mine on Thursday to go over our ratings of the jury pool members and settle on a final list of those we favored the most and the least. The bulk of the candidates were in between in the non-committal category.

Friday Kaya Kobotie called me. "David, the Attorney General insisted I give him a yes or no so I've accepted the position as the U.S. Attorney for the District of Arizona. You offered me a wonderful opportunity in the private sector but the perception of a conflict of interest would've always been there."

"I support your decision, Kaya. And I wish you nothing but the best. The State's citizens are lucky to have you administering federal laws instead of Thomas Sloan."

"Thanks. Is Ned Johnson willing to go for the voluntary manslaughter offer?"

"No. He's as adamant as ever for me to seek an acquittal."

Kaya uttered a few words I didn't understand then said, "That was 'so long I hope to see you soon' in the Hopi language."

"So long to you, Ms. United States Attorney."

Jarrett, Jim, and I returned to Mr. K's for barbecue on Saturday.

And Sunday I asked them to have dinner without me. They weren't surprised. My usual custom was to be by myself the night before the beginning of a trial and I drove the Land Rover to the Coronado National Forest and took a two-lane, winding road toward the top of Mt. Lemmon, nine-thousand feet above sea level. During the hour-long journey I passed giant Saguaro cactus, sage-brush, an array of windblown rock formations, and a forest of pine and fir trees.

I pulled off the road in the village of Summerhaven at eighty-two hundred feet to admire the vista as I ruminated on the impending bout with the federal government.

Impulsively, I called Ned on his cell phone and when he answered I said, "It's David. You're on my mind, Ned. What are you doing right now?"

"Sitting on a rock in the desert and thinking about tomorrow. Emily's at a board meeting."

"I'm thinking about tomorrow too from my vantage point near the top of Mount Lemmon."

"Our different views may give us a total picture. What do you see?"

"A hard-fought final act."

"I see victory. You've proven how good you are and I can't imagine the prosecutor beating you."

"Jurors are unpredictable, Ned."

"I understand you can't guarantee the result but a lawyer doesn't lose only one trial in almost twenty years of practice without having the ability to sway jurors to his clients' side of cases."

"You saw the *New York Times* article?"

"Emily showed it to me. You're a champ, David. With you, Jarrett, and Jim at the defense table I'm confident of my chances."

"Good night, Young Wind Runner."

"Good night, Tale Teller."

"Tale Teller?"

"Isn't that what trial attorneys do?"

"Actually, it is," I said then filled and smoked a pipe while I composed in my mind the tale I would spin to the jurors about Ned Johnson.

When darkness fell I got a bite to eat in the Alpine Café before making the downhill trip back to Tucson.

In my nightly phone call to Felicia she wished me luck achieving justice in the trial. "Justice doesn't mean you'll win, though I know justice is always your aim."

CHAPTER THIRTEEN

Monday morning there were several satellite-dish TV vans parked in front of the courthouse and more than twice as many reporters as usual were in the hallway outside Judge Warren's courtroom.

Inside, every seat in the gallery was filled. Emily, Charlie Wilson and four of his student interns occupied all the spaces on the bench behind the defense table.

Ned looked resplendent in his uniform with shiny lieutenant bars on his broad shoulders, and ribbons, including the one for bravery, on his broad chest.

As Jarrett, Jim, and I took our seats at the table I gave Axelrod and Metcalf a nod of greeting then asked Ned if he was nervous.

"A little."

"Understandable. Picking a jury should occupy your mind and ease your anxiety. If you have strong feelings about any of the candidates, pro or con, write me a note on my yellow pad. Jim gathered considerable information on them but we'll still depend heavily on our instincts in selecting a panel. We have ten peremptory challenges we can use to dismiss a candidate without expressing any reason. And we're allowed unlimited challenges for cause but the judge will rule if they're justified or not."

Court was convened and Axelrod said, "Your Honor, the Government objects to the defendant wearing his uniform to court. He'll improperly convey a sense of authority and credibility to the jury."

"Your Honor, I'm sure some of the Government's witnesses will wear their uniforms to court too and Lieutenant Johnson has as much right as they do to present himself in the best possible light."

"The Government doesn't agree," Axelrod said. "We understand he was suspended from duty when he was arrested."

"True but he's still an employee of the reservation's police department. He's on paid administrative leave."

"In that case we withdraw our objection, Your Honor."

"Then we can move on. Bailiff, please bring in the first group of jury candidates."

The bailiff went out a rear door and came back in with fourteen people who took chairs in the jury box.

The tags on their chests bore juror numbers instead of their names and they'd been chosen at random so their numbers weren't in order. But I was able to identify them on the spreadsheet in my lap top. They were a carpenter, an executive with Fry's grocery stores, a high-school teacher, a massage therapist, an attorney, a kitchen designer, a private nurse, a Veterans Administration claims officer, a prison guard, a psychologist, two homemakers, an outdoor sign painter, and a college student. None of the four Indians added to the jury pool were in the first group. The private nurse and one of the homemakers were black. All the rest were white.

Warren said, "Good morning to you Ladies and Gentlemen in the box and to the other ninety jury pool members watching and listening on closed-circuit TV in the jury conference room. The case you may be chosen to serve on is the United States of America versus Ned Johnson, the defendant. Hereinafter I will refer to the United States of America as the Government or the prosecution. The prosecution indicted the defendant for second-degree murder. An indictment is not evidence of anything. It is simply the description of charges brought by the Government. The defendant pleaded not guilty to the accusation and is presumed innocent unless those of you selected as jurors unanimously find the Government proves his guilt beyond a reasonable doubt.

"All of you candidates in the box and the jury conference room please raise your right hands. Do you solemnly swear to answer truthfully under the penalty of perjury the questions the lawyers and I ask in determining your qualifications to render a fair and unbiased verdict in this case?"

They affirmed their oaths and Warren said, "The Government is represented by Douglas Axelrod and Linda Metcalf. The defendant is represented by David Armstrong, Jarrett Hudson, and James Brown. Are any of you acquainted with these lawyers?"

None of the candidates responded but when Warren inquired into possible hardships to serving on the jury the attorney said he was due to start a trial on Wednesday and was excused. The college student said she would lose her part-time job if she served on the jury but the judge ordered her to remain.

The private nurse said she was caring for a terminally ill patient in the patient's home and was excused. The sign painter said he had billboard work he needed to finish. He was ordered to remain.

The attorney was replaced by a white female dress shop owner and the Apache set designer came in to take the seat vacated by the private nurse.

They both told Judge Warren they wouldn't be inconvenienced by serving and he said, "We'll begin the process of finding twelve jurors and two alternates who can weigh the evidence in the trial without bias and render a just verdict. Do any of you have an opinion about this case from what you've seen, read, or heard in the media?"

No one indicated they did.

"The defendant works and resides on the Tohono O'odham reservation. Do any of you have any feelings about this Indian tribe?"

No one indicated they did.

"Of any Indian tribe?"

No one indicated they did.

"Do all of you think you can judge the defendant fairly?"

Every one of the candidates nodded affirmatively and Warren continued posing general questions.

Finally, he said, "I'll let the defense make their inquiries now. You have twenty minutes, Mr. Armstrong."

I went to the lectern and said, "Thank you, Your Honor, and greetings, jury candidates. Why are we here? The police wouldn't have arrested the defendant unless they believed he was guilty. The prosecutor wouldn't have charged the defendant with murder unless he believed he was guilty. And the judge must believe there's sufficient evidence against the defendant or he would've thrown the case out of court. Right?

"Wrong. In many instances defendants have committed no crime. This happens due to faulty eye witness identification, tunnel vision detectives, bad forensic science, government-biased experts, and overzealous prosecutors. Remember the Duke Lacrosse Team players accused of gang rape not long ago? The proof against them appeared so overwhelming they were thrown off the team and expelled from the University. Then their lawyers discovered the complainant failed a lie detector test and none of the DNA samples from her vagina matched the DNA of the lacrosse players so the case was dismissed. And the ambitious District Attorney who pressed the charge lost his job and his license to practice law.

"I tell you all this to emphasize the importance of keeping an open mind and being candid when we question your qualifications to serve on the jury. It's totally understandable for you to be overawed in a federal court.

Although I've tried cases for many years, I'm still awed too. But with my client's freedom at stake I'll insist you be more forthcoming with me than you were with the judge. The questions I'll ask you aren't intended to discomfit you. Their purpose is to determine which type of case you're best suited to sit on. Because of different life experiences and personalities some of you may find another case is a better fit. So please don't try to hide your true feelings and opinions."

"I'll speak up," volunteered the Mexican male VA bureaucrat. "I believe my job makes me unusually qualified to be a juror. As a Decision Review Officer, I'm responsible for deciding if a veteran's claim was correctly assessed. To do that, I have to weigh the merits of both sides of a case before reaching a decision, just as I'll have to do here."

"Thank you for your comments."

I made eye contact with the white female Fry's executive. "Did you really intend to leave us with the impression you haven't been affected by the extensive publicity surrounding this highly controversial case?"

"No. The coverage has been unavoidable."

I looked at the white female college student. "Tell us the impression media reports have left you with."

"The defendant is a cop on the Tohono O'odham reservation and he caught the Mexican drug smugglers who killed his parents and raped and killed his sister. One got away but he shot the other one, tied him up, and took him out in the desert to be torn apart by animals."

"Do you feel Lieutenant's Johnson's actions were justified?" I asked the white female dress shop owner.

"I don't know yet. I'll decide if I'm chosen to hear all the evidence."

"How about you?" I asked the white male high-school teacher.

"I'll listen to what he has to say for himself but to my mind torture is hard to justify."

"It's important for all of you to forget about the media descriptions of what occurred in this case. Mark Twain famously said the only thing he believed in a newspaper was the date. Ned is not accused of torture. That allegation was withdrawn."

I looked at the psychologist and asked if he believed Ned was required to explain his actions.

"No. I believe defendants have the right to remain silent."

"Can any of the rest of you think of another reason why a defendant wouldn't want to take the stand?"

"Yeah," said the white male prison guard. "He's paying you to be his mouthpiece and you don't want to risk the Government lawyers getting the truth out of him."

I turned my attention the female black homemaker. "The judge said the indictment against Lieutenant Johnson doesn't prove anything. Do you agree?"

"In a sense but I can't ignore what he did and I think the Government was right to charge him with a crime."

The male Apache set designer said. "Ridding his Nation of a pest wasn't a crime and it's about time other Indians take the same stance. We've let intruders interfere in our affairs way too long."

I addressed the group. "Let's talk about what the indictment means. If someone accuses us of doing something, our reaction is to say prove it. That's true in a legal sense too. The burden is on the prosecution to substantiate every element of their charge beyond a reasonable doubt. The defendant has no burden to establish his innocence. If the prosecution fails to meet their burden, is the defendant entitled to go free," I asked the white female homemaker.

"I believe that's the way the system works."

I faced the white male carpenter. "What would the Government need to build a bridge, sir?"

"Steel, cable, and concrete I guess."

"What would happen if they left the cables out?" I asked the white female massage therapist.

"I suppose the bridge would fail."

I turned to the white male sign painter. "Will the prosecution's case fail if they don't prove every element of their charge beyond a reasonable doubt?"

"It would have to."

"Isn't that the standard you'd want to be tried by if you're ever alleged to have committed a crime?" I asked the kitchen designer.

"Sure. Nobody wants to be pre-judged."

"I appreciate the candor you've all shown me and to those of you who end up on the panel I make this promise—when all the evidence is in and all the witnesses have been heard you'll understand the killing of the drug smuggler by Lieutenant Johnson was justifiable homicide."

I sat down and Axelrod stepped over to the lectern. He didn't engage the individual candidates as much as I had but he effectively used his allotted time to communicate the Government's position.

Judge Warren declared a fifteen minute recess.

CHAPTER FOURTEEN

I told Emily and Charlie that Ned, Jarrett, Jim, and I needed to stay at the table and consider which of the candidates we wanted to remove so they left with the interns, saying they'd bring us back coffee from the cafeteria.

Ned said, "David, I already told you how I feel about the Apache and my heart won't be broken if you get rid of the prison guard too."

Jim said, "Axelrod will presumably challenge the Apache for cause and we can challenge the guard, the black homemaker, and the high-school teacher. I recommend we dismiss the VA officer as well, David. He tried to ingratiate himself with both you and Axelrod and I'm thinking he has a secret agenda. Not to mention he's Mexican and might disapprove of Ned killing the drug smuggler."

"He hasn't said anything to justify a challenge for cause and using a peremptory on a racial minority is *verboten*."

Emily and Charlie returned with our cups of coffee and after Jarrett took a sip of his he said, "Most of the rest of candidates are lemmings who will unfailingly follow the leaders."

"The leaders being the grocery chain executive and the psychologist?" I asked.

"Yes. I think the VA officer is an unknown; the prison guard, the high-school teacher, and the carpenter favor the prosecution; the Apache set designer and the dress shop owner favor the defense; and the lemmings are the college girl, the two homemakers, the massage therapist, the kitchen designer, and the sign painter."

I asked Jim and Ned if they went along with Jarrett. They nodded and I said I'd act accordingly.

82

Following the recess Judge Warren said, "Counsels, I'll entertain your challenges at a sidebar before I have the jury candidates brought back in."

We approached the bench and Warren told me to go first.

"Your Honor, the defense challenges the prison guard for cause. His comments demonstrated a bias against Lieutenant Johnson and an indication of his cynical attitude about the trial process."

"Challenge accepted. Next."

"The defense challenges the high-school teacher for cause. He expressed a pre-disposed mindset against Lieutenant Johnson."

"Challenge denied."

"Then I exercise a peremptory."

"Challenge accepted. Next."

"Our final challenge is the black homemaker for saying Lieutenant Johnson must be guilty of something or the Government wouldn't have indicted him."

"Challenge accepted. Mr. Axelrod?"

"The Government challenges the Apache set designer for cause, Your Honor. His responses revealed unmistakable support for the defendant's actions."

"Challenge accepted. Next."

"We peremptorily challenge the dress shop owner and the psychologist, Your Honor."

"I'll dismiss them. You may return to your tables."

Once the candidates were in the jury box again Judge Warren said, "Juror Numbers Seventeen, Forty-Four, Seventy-Nine, Eighty, Eighty-Eight, and Ninety-Three are excused and can return to the jury assembly room. The lawyers felt you weren't suited for this particular case. Thank you for your service to the community."

Five of the six rejected candidates departed without fanfare but the Apache grumbled on his way out. "White man's justice is justice denied."

The bailiff escorted the replacements in. They were a black male Tucson City Works mechanic, a white female bank branch manager, a white male swimming pool salesman, a white female State Park Ranger, a white male programming manager at Raytheon Missile Systems, and a white female Wal-Mart clerk.

None of the new candidates claimed service would be a hardship and Judge Warren, Axelrod, and I took turns questioning them.

By the end of the afternoon session the City Works mechanic was replaced by a white female restaurant hostess. The park ranger was replaced by a white female postal worker. And the Wal-Mart clerk was replaced by a white male long-haul truck driver.

Before Judge Warren adjourned the proceedings he instructed the candidates to not discuss the case with anyone, including their families and friends, and to refrain from exposing themselves to any news coverage of the trial.

Emily, Ned, Charlie, Jarrett, Jim, and I went out the rear exit of the lobby to escape the reporters' attention and found a nearby bar to have drinks and discuss the session.

Ned took a swallow of his apple juice and said, "I'm feeling pretty good about the people currently in the jury box with the exception of the VA officer. Ever since we talked about him at the break I've been wondering why he's trying so hard to be on the jury. Most people look for ways to avoid jury service."

He worries me too," I said. "But I've explained how difficult it is to strike a member of a racial minority."

Jim said, "Which is odd since race is the very reason we don't want him on the panel. He's Mexican and there's a chance he's concealing his sympathy for the drug smuggler Ned killed."

"It's also odd I'm perceived as hostile to Mexicans," Ned said. "The Tohono O'odham reservation extends into Sonora, Mexico and all of us on this side of the border have relatives and ancient ties on the other side. What I did to the drug smuggler is what I would've done to a man of any race who killed my family. How do we handle the VA officer, David?"

"We wait and hope he slips up when he's answering questions. I'll delve into fresh areas during tomorrow's *voir dire* and try to draw him out."

Charlie commented on the predominance of whites in the jury pool and Jim predicted we'd have a jury by the end of Tuesday's session.

We finished our drinks and walked back to our cars in the courthouse garage.

Jarrett, Jim, and I continued discussing the problem of the VA claims officer during dinner later.

I said, "He poses a real conflict for me. My duty to zealously defend a client includes choosing the very best jury I can. But if the VA counselor doesn't say something to give me grounds to challenge him for cause, I'll be derelict in my duty if I don't try to peremptorily challenge him and that could subject me to discipline by the Bar for engaging in purposeful racial discrimination."

We couldn't come up with an easy way out of my dilemma and I hoped Felicia didn't pick up the strain I was under when I called her from the suite before I retired for the night.

CHAPTER FIFTEEN

At breakfast the next morning Jim said, "I ran more searches on the VA officer, last night, David. Nothing new popped up until I keyed him in by his last name only and saw an article in *USA Today* about the shooting of an unarmed Mexican drug runner named Jorge Rodriguez by two Border Patrol Agents in Laredo, Texas last year. The agents were indicted for murder but released after two trials ended in hung juries. Jorge was only twenty years old and the article quoted a statement his older brother, Javier, made to the Tucson *Daily Star*. I sent the article to Jarrett and you but you probably haven't checked your emails today. I suggest you do."

Jarrett and I turned on our lap tops and when I read the article I said, "You're worth your weight in gold, Jim. We now know the VA officer does have a secret agenda but how the hell did he manage to get in the jury pool for Ned's trial. A long time ago Abe taught me to never believe in coincidence. He said if vultures start hanging out near your abode they're not there by chance. They're there waiting for you to die."

Jim said, "Maybe you can reach the jury commissioner before we're due in court and ask about Rodriguez. You spoke to her about the lack of Indian representation before you left New York so she'll probably remember who you are. I just brought up the site online. Their office opens at seven a.m. and it's already a quarter past eight."

"Good idea," I replied and called the office on my cell phone.

The commissioner was in and after I described the situation she asked me to hold for a few minutes. When she came back on the line she gave me the information I requested.

I thanked her and told Jarrett and Jim it was time for us to go the courthouse and see Rodriguez's head roll. "He volunteered to serve in the current jury pool. The commissioner says he contacted her clerk, told her he was due vacation time, knew many people didn't respond to jury summonses, and would like to perform his civic duty in their place."

"I didn't think you could volunteer for jury service," Jim said.

"Candidates are chosen at random to sit on juries but you can volunteer for the pool."

"The slimy bastard should be tried himself for attempting to corrupt the system."

When we got to the courtroom I whispered the news to Ned, Emily, and Charlie then alerted Axelrod and asked the clerk for a chambers conference with the judge.

She called him on the intercom, the court reporter took her machine through the door to his office, and the bailiff said counsels could go in too.

Once our party and Axelrod and Metcalf were situated in front of Warren's desk he said, "Why are we here, Mr. Armstrong?"

"Your Honor, the defense has discovered Juror Number Thirteen, Javier Rodriguez, has given dishonest replies to questions in *voir dire*. I thought it best to confront him in private rather than in the presence of the other candidates."

Warren agreed and asked his secretary to have the bailiff bring Rodriguez in.

The VA officer was ushered into the office and the judge commanded him to take a seat. "Mr. Armstrong has some concerns to address with you."

"Thank you, Your Honor. Mr. Rodriguez, our investigator has come up with some troubling information about you …"

Rodriguez turned to the judge. "You told us no one but you and court personnel would know our names."

"No. I said I would order court personnel and the lawyers to keep your identities confidential. That didn't mean the lawyers couldn't access public records to see if anything might disqualify you from serving as jurors. Continue, Mr. Armstrong."

"Mr. Rodriguez, do you recall Judge Warren asking you and the other candidates if you knew anyone involved in smuggling drugs from Mexico?"

"Yes."

"What did you say?"

"I didn't respond."

"Even though your younger brother, Jorge, was killed by two Border Patrol agents while trying to bring marijuana into Laredo, Texas?"

"I … I … I'm not sure why I didn't speak up."

"Was it because you wanted to conceal your bias against Lieutenant

Johnson to better your chances of being picked for the jury so you could influence this trial?"

Rodriguez hesitated to answer and I said, "I'll put the question to you more directly. Was it because you're enraged the Border Patrol agents were freed after two juries failed to reach verdicts?"

The VA employee continued to maintain his silence and I said, "I'll read the statement you gave the *Tucson Star* after the second mistrial of the agents: 'I'm a Mexican-American citizen and I've worked for our federal government most of my adult life but I'm ashamed our justice department has a policy of letting Border Patrol officers act with virtual impunity when dealing with illegal immigrants and smugglers from Mexico. And I'm ashamed American jurors apparently think law enforcement personnel are above the law.' Is that a correct quote, Mr. Rodriguez?"

"Yes," he said defiantly.

Judge Warren, "You're dismissed, sir. Leave from court rather than through the jury room. I don't want you talking with the other pool members. I'll instruct the jury commissioner to remove you from the jury rolls so you'll never again be called for duty. And I'll send a transcript of this meeting to the acting U.S. Attorney for her to decide whether to charge you with perjury."

Rodriguez left without apologizing and Judge Warren told the rest of us we could return to our tables.

The session was called to order and Judge Warren spoke to the fourteen people in the jury box. "Good morning, Ladies and Gentlemen. Juror Number Thirteen has been dismissed. Juror Number Twenty-Five has joined us in his place."

I looked at the spreadsheet in my lap top and noted the replacement candidate was a Ford dealership owner. I further noted he was a deacon in the Mormon Church.

In federal criminal trials the prosecution is only allowed six peremptory challenges. By the afternoon break Axelrod had spent his remaining four by getting rid of the restaurant hostess, the swimming pool salesman, the massage therapist, and the homemaker.

Their substitutions were a retired white male FBI agent, a white female day care operator, a white male ranch hand, and a white female accountant.

I used two of my nine remaining peremptory challenges on the Mormon auto dealer and another on the retired FBI agent after the judge didn't accept my challenges of them for cause.

They were replaced by another white female homemaker and a white male turquoise jewelry maker.

Neither Axelrod nor I found any cause to challenge the new candidates and I was tempted to accept the panel.

However, after consultation with my tablemates I took the chance of getting Indian pool members on the jury and used peremptories on the day care operator and the accountant.

The first replacement was a white female accountant and, lo and behold, the second was an Indian woman.

I looked at Ned and he said, "She's the Tohono O'odham nurse for sure, David. You won the gamble."

The victory was short-lived. When the judge asked her if she could be fair and impartial she said, "I'll try but I would be less than honest if I didn't tell you I think Lieutenant Johnson should never have been charged with a crime."

Warren dismissed her and after the next candidate, a white female dentist, passed our muster we impaneled a jury.

Judge Warren said, "Congratulations, Ladies and Gentlemen. You've all made the final cut. Raise your right hands. Does each of you swear under the penalty of perjury to render a verdict in this matter based on nothing but the evidence presented and the instructions of the court?"

A unanimous chorus of "I do's" followed then Warren said, "We'll adjourn early today. As soon as you go to the deliberation room and elect a foreperson you can go home. The foreperson will occupy the first chair in the jury box every day. The rest of you may take the remaining seats as you see fit but always sit in the same order. Remember not to discuss the case with anyone and refrain from reading, hearing, or watching news coverage of the trial. Court is adjourned until nine a.m. tomorrow."

Charlie said he knew the very place for us to celebrate picking a jury.

The Tucson Project's interns said goodbye and my tablemates, Emily, and I followed Charlie out of the courthouse and down a side street to the Surly Wench, a pub featuring a long bar, images of scantily clad "wenches" on the walls, and free pool tables. The food and drink menus advertised live music nightly, striptease shows on weekends, and a sign on the wall spelled out the establishment's credo: THIS PLACE IS A BAR FOR ALMOST EVERYBODY. STRAIGHTS, GAYS, COWBOYS, INDIANS, BIKERS, HIPPIES, AND PEOPLE OF ANY COLOR ARE WELCOME. THE ONLY PEOPLE WE DON'T WANT HERE ARE THOSE WHO MESS WITH OTHER PATRONS' HAPPINESS.

The beers and well drinks were reasonably priced and we all ordered scotches on the rocks except for Ned and Emily who asked for drafts of Gold Creek Lager, an Arizona microbrewery brand.

Charlie said, "I think the jury is well-balanced even though no Indians made the panel."

"We could've done worse," I said. "Remind us who our twelve citizens are, Jarrett."

"The Fry's executive, the jewelry maker, the postal worker, the carpenter, the ranch hand, the bank branch manager, the bus dispatcher, the long-haul truck driver, the Raytheon manager, the college girl, the kitchen designer, and the sign painter."

Jim looked at his lap top screen. "Six males, six females, eleven Caucasians and one Mexican-American. There's an even split between white and blue collar jobs. Most of the panelists have so-called normal sexual orientations but I'd bet a pretty penny the jewelry maker is gay. Finally, in running background reports on them I didn't find any with political leanings extreme enough to cause us any concerns."

"Then you guy weren't just crap guessing," Emily said.

"No. There was a method to our madness," I said, "or perhaps madness to our method but we weren't acting blindly. Despite what potential jurors may say to the contrary, the media coverage of a high-profile trial prejudices them against a defendant so we tried to get rid of the candidates we perceived as intractable and kept those we believed we had some chance of swaying to Ned's side. The process is more a matter of de-selection than selection, though the rule against race-based challenges prevented me from getting rid of the Mexican-American ranch hand."

Charlie said, "You could've paid a jury consultant thousands of dollars and not achieved a better result."

"In my opinion, jury selection is an art, not a science, and most trial attorneys are the best practitioners of the art."

"On that note, I'll take my leave," Charlie said.

Ned and Emily were ready to go too but Jarrett, Jim, and I opted to stay for another drink and ended up having plates of mini-burgers for an early dinner.

The 'sliders' served to a patron at a nearby table looked and smelled so good we had to try them. We were glad we did. They were greasy but so delectable we got into a contest to see who could eat the most. Jim wolfed down eleven and won easily.

After Jarrett and Jim volunteered to have the Radisson's Business Center print out the documents we'd need in court the next day we separated for the evening and I smoked a pipe on the balcony of my suite as I considered what I would say to the jury. Because surveys of jurors after trials have shown approximately eighty-five percent of them make up their minds about a case during the opening statements of the lawyers I always tried to make my beginning remarks as dramatic and convincing as possible. However, to prevent sounding stale I never memorized a speech. I just wrote notes to remind me of the key points I wanted to make.

I went through three bowlfuls of tobacco and two more scotches before I was satisfied enough with my approach to call Felicia then take a shower and go to bed.

CHAPTER SIXTEEN

Wednesday I awoke early and opened the front door of the suite to bring in my freshly shined shoes and the morning edition of the *Star*.

The front page of the newspaper featured an article on the trial I ignored but I did check out the weather report on the upper right hand corner and see the forecast was for another sunny and hot day in Tucson.

For appearances in the Supreme Court and other appellate tribunals I wore dark tailor-made suits from London with power-red ties. For trials off the rack was just fine and I chose a Brooks Brothers light blue seersucker suit, with white dress shirt, and club tie.

I met Jarrett and Jim in the café for breakfast before driving us to the federal courthouse.

The *Times* reporter, Cindy Hill, was in the hallway outside Judge Warren's courtroom but she didn't try to impede my progress and neither did her colleagues, perhaps because she'd warned them how irascible I could be when media representatives bothered me during a trial.

I was glad to see Drew Peterson, the public defender, sitting on the bench with Emily, Charlie, and three Project interns.

"I took vacation to watch you perform your magic," Drew explained to me.

"I'll make sure I still have a rabbit in my hat. I don't want to disappoint you."

I got the usual hug from Emily and the fist bump from Ned. He stood erect in his uniform and I could see a positive attitude in his brown eyes.

Charlie asked if I was reading Cindy Hill's trial reports in the *Times* and I said, "Not since the first one. I barely have time to read the paperwork associated with the case. Is Cindy continuing to trumpet me as the reincarnation of Clarence Darrow?"

"Pretty much. She's obviously impressed with you but her accounts of the trial sessions are insightful and informative."

The judge came in and his bailiff yelled, "All rise. The United States District Court for the District of Arizona, the Honorable Vaughn Warren presiding in the matter of <u>U.S. vs. Ned Johnson</u>, is now in session."

Warren motioned us back in our seats and the jurors filed into the box. The Fry's grocery chain executive took the first chair indicating she was the foreperson.

"Good morning, Ladies and Gentlemen. I want to take a few minutes to describe your responsibilities as jurors and to give you some instructions. At the end of the trial I'll give you more detailed instructions.

"It will be your duty to decide from the evidence what the facts are. You and you alone, are the judges of the facts. You will hear the evidence, decide what the facts are, and apply those facts to the law I read to you. That is how you will reach your verdict. In doing so you must follow the law whether you agree with it or not. You should not take anything I may say during the trial as an inference of what I think of the evidence or what your verdict should be.

"The defendant is charged with murder in the second-degree. In order for the defendant to be found guilty of the charge, the Government must prove several specific elements beyond a reasonable doubt. I will give you instructions on these elements before you retire for deliberations.

"To insure fairness you jurors must obey the following rules: Do not talk among yourselves about the case until the end of the trial when you go to the jury room to decide on a verdict. Do not talk with anyone else, including your family and friends, about the case. Do not speak to any of the witnesses or lawyers—you should not even pass the time of day with them. If a party from one side sees you talking to a party from the other side, an unwarranted suspicion about your fairness might arise. Do not read any news stories or listen to any radio or television reports about the case. Do not do any research about the case on your own. Do not make up your mind about what the verdict should be until after all the evidence has been presented and you are deliberating. Keep an open mind until then.

"The first step in the trial will be the opening statements. The lawyers for the Government and the defense will tell you the evidence they intend to introduce. Next the Government will offer their evidence through witnesses and exhibits. After the Government rests, the defense may put on their case but they're not required to do so. The defendant doesn't have to prove his innocence. Under the law he is presumed innocent unless the Government meets their burden to prove their charges beyond a reasonable doubt. After you've heard from both sides the Government and defense will deliver their final arguments. The last part of the trial occurs when I instruct you on the rules of law you are to follow in reaching a verdict and you leave the courtroom to make your decision. Your deliberations will be secret. You will never have to explain your verdict to anyone. We will now hear the prosecution's opening statement."

Axelrod said, "This is a very simple case so I will be short and to the point, Jurors. We will prove the defendant shot the victim and left him in the desert to die from a combination of the gunshot wound and attacks by wild animals. The latter action negates any defense of justified homicide. The victim deserved to be punished for the terrible crimes he committed against defendant's family but not even the worst of the worst offenders deserves to be eaten alive by predators. Thank you."

"Mr. Armstrong will now deliver the defense's opening statement.

Instead of going to the lectern I stood, asked Ned to stand too, and put my hand on his shoulder. "My colleagues and I are proud to represent this man, Ladies and Gentlemen. The media coverage of his case has been extensive in Tucson and beyond but I'm here to tell you parts of the story you'll hear for the first time. Ned was born and raised on the Tohono O'odham reservation. He was an honor student and star athlete in high school, served with distinction and bravery in the first Iraq conflict, returned to become one of the highest ranking officers in the tribal police department, and is such a respected member of the Tohono O'odham Nation a medicine man chose to teach him the sacred and secret traditions of his people.

"Before I continue I need to be sure you're aware of a major problem on the reservation. The Border Patrol erected a steel fence to prevent entry by vehicles from the Southern border so Mexican men, women, and children immigrants are now trying to walk across the desert in the reservation and dying of exposure and dehydration at the rate of thirty-five or forty a month. At the same time Mexican smugglers are bringing in marijuana on their backs and bribing and intimidating the Indian residents to drive them and their contraband north. There have been numerous incidents of the smugglers reacting violently when their demands weren't met, and of them robbing and committing other crimes against Indian residents.

"Sunday, April 30th of this year was a cloudless, hot day reaching in the nineties. Ned was off-duty and on his way to visit his family. He parked his pickup a ways from their adobe dwelling and, in keeping with tribal custom, waited for someone to open the front door and invite him to come in. No one appeared but he heard muffled screams from inside the house, took his single-shot, bolt-action rifle from the truck, and sneaked around the property to a side window. What he saw was horrifying. His mother and father lay dead on the floor, their throats cut so deeply their heads were almost severed from their bodies. His sister was still alive but one Mexican man was holding a knife to her throat and mauling her breasts while another Mexican man was violently raping her. Ned shot a round from his rifle at the man with the knife but he missed and the man ran out the back door. The rapist opened fire with an automatic pistol and Ned's second round struck the rapist in the stomach. As the rapist sagged to the floor he continued firing his pistol and several bullets struck Ned's sister in the chest. Ned rushed in to help her but she died in his arms. Overcome with grief and anger, he tied up the barely conscious Mexican, put him in the bed of his pickup, drove into the desert, secured the man's wrists and ankles to stakes in the ground, and left him. Ned then continued on to Sells and told his police chief what had occurred. Until that moment Ned had never been arrested for any crime, not even minor traffic offenses, nor had any suspect ever accused him of abuse."

I let Ned sit down and made my way to the lectern. "I can imagine how Ned seeing the bodies of his murdered parents and witnessing the rape of his sister caused him to take such a cruel action but I can't imagine what I would've done if I were in his moccasins, so to speak. Can you imagine what you would've done if your family was wiped out by a couple of hateful drug smugglers?"

Most of the jurors shook their heads and I continued. "Now that I've established what happened I'll address the legal ramifications. Under the law Ned, like every other citizen, has a right to use deadly force to stop a felony in progress and prevent harm to himself or other persons as long as the force is reasonable under the circumstances. In Ned's case shooting to kill was undeniably reasonable since his single-shot rifle was overmatched by the Mexican's automatic pistol. I'm sure the prosecutor and I are in agreement on this point. Where we differ is on Ned's secondary action. The prosecutor argued that leaving the man helpless in the desert to endure attacks constituted unreasonable force. And when the prosecutor presents his case I have no doubt he will appeal to your emotions by showing you grisly photographs of the Mexican's ravaged body and pointing out the missing eyes, the fingers eaten to the bone, and the open chest cavity revealing the missing lungs and heart which were presumably eaten by predators.

"I can't deny those attacks were awful but our expert, who is considered the world's foremost authority on forensic pathology, will tell you the animal attacks occurred after the Mexican was already dead from the gunshot wound.

I thank you for your attention and look forward to talking to you again after all the evidence is in."

Axelrod frowned at me as I passed his table on the way to mine.

CHAPTER SEVENTEEN

The judge recessed court for fifteen minutes and Drew said, "David, your opening argument appeared to perturb the prosecutor. Anytime we lawyers rile our opponents we know we've hit a home run."

"Your baseball analogy is apt. When Yogi Berra was managing the Yankees he was asked why he constantly tried to get under the skin of other managers. In one of his funny malapropisms Berra said, 'If you get them angry, they'll make too many wrong mistakes.' I think the same is true in a courtroom."

Emily said, "I was impressed by how clearly you explained a complicated case, David. Boiling the facts down to a question of whether or not the Mexican was dead when the desert creatures preyed on his body gives the jurors an easy way to reach a verdict."

Charlie agreed. "I think Axelrod was also irked at you telling the jurors what to expect when he shows them the photos of the Mexican's corpse."

"It was also Axelrod's first inkling of our forensic expert's finding, which, if accepted by the jury, will destroy the Government's case. What did you think of my opening, Ned?"

"I thought you were real good, Tale Teller. I feel like the door to my freedom is already half way open."

"That's Ned's new name for me. He says I tell tales to jurors."

"If he means tall tales, he's right on," said Jim.

"And then some," said Jarrett.

Ned said, "From now on your name is Tall-Tale Teller, David."

"As long as I don't have to go through a painful initiation ordeal I accept the revised moniker with honor but let's get back to business. The trial is moving fast and you should alert our witnesses on the reservation to come to the courthouse tomorrow and be available to testify. Jim, you should also arrange for Colonel Long to be here."

"I'm ahead of you. He's arriving on a U.S. Air flight at seven tonight and I booked him a room in a boutique hotel a block away from here. As a special surprise I've arranged for a hooker to appear at his door after dinner."

"Jim!"

"Okay. I'll scratch the hooker but haven't you heard the refrain—old soldiers never die, they just fade away in the throes of passion."

I was saved from answering by the bailiff calling for order again and Axelrod putting Chief Rivas on the stand.

The clerk swore in Rivas and Axelord asked him to state his occupation.

"I'm chief of the Tohono O'odham Police Department."

"Chief Rivas, on the 30th of April this year did Ned Johnson, a lieutenant in the Department, give you information regarding the murders of his parents and sister? Yes or no?"

"Yes."

"Did Lieutenant Johnson say he wounded and apprehended a Mexican drug smuggler he believed responsible for the murders. Yes or no?"

"Yes."

"Did he also tell you he left the Mexican drug smuggler in the desert to die? Yes or no?"

"Yes."

"What did you do?"

"I reported the information to the FBI agent in charge of the Tucson office."

"Couldn't you have responded to the information on your own authority?"

"No. The FBI has jurisdiction over major crimes committed on the reservation. We sometimes help them investigate major crimes and gather evidence for them but the responsibility is theirs."

"Chief Rivas I hand you this report and ask if you're familiar with it."

"I am. I wrote the report."

"Note that several portions are blacked out due to a ruling by the judge. That's why I was so careful in my initial questions to you."

"I'm aware of the redactions."

"Your Honor, I offer Chief Rivas's report for identification as Government Exhibit One and ask for its admission in evidence."

"Request granted."

"Chief, how did you respond to the information?"

"I dispatched officers to the Johnson family's house and to the place the lieutenant said he left the Mexican's body to protect the scenes until the FBI's evidence response team arrived. I also contacted the county medical examiner's office and asked them to send out one of their pathologists. But since one of our officers was involved I refrained from ordering any investigation by my department's personnel to avoid any appearance of a conflict of interest."

"Did an FBI agent arrest Lieutenant Johnson and charge him with shooting the Mexican and leaving him in the desert to die?"

"Yes."

"I have no further questions of this witness for the moment, Your Honor."

"Mr. Armstrong?"

"Thank you, Your Honor, and good morning, Chief Rivas. Do you have a personal relationship with Lieutenant Johnson?"

"Yes. We're close. Ned's like a son to me."

"Then this must be hard for you."

"Very hard. When Elder Brother created Ned Johnson he threw the formula away. They don't come any better than him. I'm sorry for the predicament he's in and wish there was a way I could help him."

"Thank you for telling us, sir."

"Re-direct, Mr. Axelrod?"

"Chief Rivas, despite your relationship with the defendant you do think he should be held liable for criminal actions like anyone else, don't you?"

"Yes but I'm not sure what Ned did was criminal. I believe he was fully justified in shooting the Mexican. As for leaving him in the desert, I guess we need to know what Ned's frame of mind was. Seeing his family slaughtered was quite a blow and he might easily have been temporarily deprived of reason."

Axelrod was obviously unhappy with the answer but rather than risk hearing another, even more damaging one, he sat down.

I didn't have any other questions for the chief either and Axelrod called FBI Special Agent Susan Cuzic to the stand.

She was wearing jeans and a polo shirt. "Your Honor, I apologize for coming to court in casual attire. My team is on call today."

"Not a problem, Agent Cuzic."

Axelrod said, "Are you assigned to the FBI's Tucson office, Agent Cuzic?"

"Yes, sir."

"What are your responsibilities?"

"I'm the leader of one of our two evidence response teams. We have two to enable us to respond twenty-four-seven. When a federal case requires a complex crime scene search or the use of specialized forensic technology, members of the ERT are immediately deployed. We also assist local law enforcement agencies upon request."

"Please tell us your background and education."

"I was born and raised in Washington, D.C. My father is an assistant FBI Director and the day I reached the minimum required age of twenty-three I was hired by the Agency myself, achieving a lifelong ambition. By then I had a B.S. degree in computer science from Georgetown University and later earned a law degree there. During an assignment in the Sandusky, Ohio office I obtained a Masters in Criminal Justice from Tiffin University and, like all members of evidence recovery teams, I've received extensive instruction in advanced forensic techniques at the FBI Academy."

"Is every member of your team an agent?"

"No, sir. Ten of us are agents and six of us are civilian support employees with specialized knowledge and skills."

"When were you ordered to investigate the murders in this case?"

"The Special Agent in charge of our office contacted me shortly before two p.m. on April 30th. Even though it was a Sunday, our team was on call so we were assembled and rolling in a couple of our Ford F-Two-Fifty's by two-thirty. One of the trucks is outfitted as our mobile crime lab. The other carried us and four ATV's in the bed."

"What preliminary information about the crimes did you have?"

"All the AIG told me was that Lieutenant Ned Johnson of the Tohono O'odham Police Department shot a Mexican drug smuggler he suspected of killing his parents and of raping and killing his sister then left the wounded man in the desert to die."

"Please describe the conduct of your investigation for the jurors."

"We arrived at the reservation's police headquarters less than sixty minutes later and Chief Rivas assigned an officer to lead us to the crime scenes. Since the body had been laying in the desert for several hours I decided we should start at that scene first. We didn't need to check the man's pulse to know he was dead. The stench of death was strong and we had to shoo away the buzzards feasting on the cadaver. We began by surveying the scene then divided up to map it in three-dimensional technology on a computer, draw sketches and diagrams of it, photograph it with video and still cameras from every angle, and record a narrative description."

"The sight of the body must've been repugnant."

"I've seen far worse but it was unpleasant."

Axelrod showed the agent a bound document. "Agent Cuzic, is this a true and accurate copy of the report you made of your investigation?"

"Yes, sir."

"Your Honor, I offer this report for identification as Government Exhibit Two and ask for its admission as evidence."

"So ordered."

"May Ms. Metcalf project on the screen the videotape listed as Attachment Eight of the report?"

"She may."

"Jurors, even though defense counsel warned I'd show you grisly images of the victim, prepare yourselves for a fright."

Jurors gasped as the videotape showed the Mexican man lying on his back with his arms and legs tethered to stakes. His clothing was in shreds, ants crawled over his skin, and flies flitted about. He had two gaping wounds—in his abdomen and in his chest—and many smaller ones. His eyes were missing, his fingers gnawed to the bone, his ears, face, and lips eaten away, and, shockingly, his jaw was frozen open in what appeared to be a cry of agony.

Axelrod motioned for Metcalf and the screen went blank. "I'm sorry, Ladies and Gentlemen, but it was important for you to see that evidence. Agent Cuzic, please continue your account of your team's investigation."

"We detected and collected latent prints. We used forensic vacuums and alternate light sources to find and collect hairs, fibers, and other trace evidence. We took samples of blood and bodily fluids from the victim's body. We made casts of shoe and boot impressions. We used metal detectors and radar to search for underground evidence. And a K9 team of dog and handler searched for evidence in general. We then went to the other crime scene—the Johnson family house—and performed all the same tasks plus the additional task of bloodstain pattern analysis. We collected much more evidence than at the desert scene. A pistol and several spent cartridges were found. Also two backpacks. And the K9 team detected a bloody knife beside a path behind the house."

"Did you come to any conclusions from your investigation, Agent Cuzic?"

"I wouldn't say conclusions. As with all crimes, I developed a general theory of what occurred based on my team's findings and on the information I obtained from interviews with the other law enforcement officers involved."

"Could you summarize your theory for us?"

"Yes, sir. I deduced Lieutenant Johnson went to the home of his father, mother, and fifteen-year old sister and saw his parents' dead bodies on the living room floor and witnessed two Mexican men attacking his sister. One man was holding a knife under her chin and the other one was raping her. Lieutenant Johnson fired his rifle at the man with the knife but missed and that man escaped out a rear door. The other man opened fire with a handgun and the lieutenant shot him in the abdomen but not before some of the man's bullets killed the sister. The lieutenant then took the wounded Mexican into the desert and left him there."

"What motive, if any, did you discern for the murders and rape?"

"I believe they were related to the invasion of the home by the Mexicans. The most likely scenario is the family returned to the house and surprised the men and they reacted by slitting the throat of Mr. and Mrs. Johnson then decided to have their way with the Johnson's young daughter. Drug smugglers on their way back to Mexico often break into homes on the reservation to steal jewelry, watches, cameras and other small articles they can trade for food and drink on their long trek home. I think that was the case with the two Mexicans. We found very little money in the dead Mexican's clothes but we did find over a hundred thousand dollars divided between the two backpacks we discovered. The bills were sewn into the linings, leading me to assume they were proceeds from a drug sale and not for the personal use of the smugglers."

"Don't most of the smugglers bring marijuana in on their backs?"

"As a rule."

"How much marijuana would they've had to carry across the border to receive a hundred thousand dollars in Arizona's wholesale drug market?"

"Not as much as you might think. At the going wholesale rate of five-hundred dollars a pound each of the two men would've only had to bring in a hundred pounds of pot, which is in keeping with the *modus operandi* of Mexican smugglers. They typically work in pairs with each of them carrying two fifty pound bags of the illegal substance."

"Have you formed an opinion as to whether the Mexican was dead or alive when wild creatures attacked his body in the desert?"

"No, sir. I read the medical examiner's findings but I'm not qualified to comment on them."

"Thanks for your testimony, Agent Cuzic. I'll turn you over to defense counsel now."

"Mr. Armstrong?"

"Thank you, Your Honor, and hello, Agent Cuzic. I appreciate your refusal to draw unwarranted assumptions from your investigation. The real world of evidence recovery isn't like the CSI TV series, is it?"

"Hardly. We don't solve crimes in thirty minutes. Sometimes we don't solve them at all. Everything is dependent on the lab tests of the evidence we gather at scenes and DNA testing seems to take forever. If the eventual results inculpate a suspect, fine. If they don't, there's nothing we can do. We've already gone on to the next cases anyway. The public perception of CSI investigators persists, though. When I tell people I meet at cocktail parties what my job is we're never at a loss for conversation."

"I wish you a continued successful career, Agent. Your father must be very proud of you."

"He is. Every time I visit him in his Hoover Building office he shows me off to other top-floor executives as if I'm the star quarterback of the Washington Redskins instead of just one of thousands of field agents toiling away in anonymity."

CHAPTER EIGHTEEN

Judge Warren declared a lunch break but I begged off going to the cafeteria with the group and was content eating a granola bar I bought from a vendor in the lobby then smoking a pipe on the street while I reviewed the notes from my conversation with Dr. Shapiro to cram for the cross-examination of the medical examiner. The lab supervisor would testify ahead of him but the ME was the witness I needed to impeach the most if I was to have any chance of the jurors acquitting Ned.

Finished with my pipe smoke, I tapped out the tobacco ashes and was walking up the steps to the courthouse entrance when a Mexican man approached me with a switchblade knife in his hand and said, "You have this coming for defending the murderer of Fabian Cruz."

As he thrust the knife blade at me I held up the yellow pad for a shield and moved backwards, slipping on the steps in the process.

The next thing I knew I was laying on a gurney in an ambulance. A paramedic said, "Keep still, Mister. You fell and banged your head and were unconscious for several minutes. We're taking you to Tucson Medical Center for an examination."

"Was I stabbed?"

"No. An FBI agent disarmed and arrested your assailant."

With siren blaring, the ambulance arrived at the hospital and I was wheeled into the emergency room and taken to a bed in a small room.

A nurse helped me take off my suit jacket, unrolled the left sleeve of my shirt, and placed a cuff from a monitoring machine around my arm.

She then treated and bandaged the bump on my head. "You've got a nasty contusion on your noggin. Is it painful to my touch?"

"A little."

"Your blood pressure and heart rate look good. Are you nauseous?"

"No."

"Dizzy?"

"No."

"What's the date?"

"Wednesday, August 10th."

"Who's the President of the United States?"

"Michelle Obama."

"Are you sure?"

"Yes. Her husband's the front man but she runs the whole show from behind the scenes."

"Okay, Smartie-Pants. There's a bottle of water on the stand if you're thirsty. Don't get out of bed until a doctor has seen you."

While I waited I thought about what the Mexican who tried to stab me said but I couldn't imagine Fabian Ruiz being important enough for the drug cartel to send a hit man to kill me.

My reverie was interrupted by the entrance of a young man. Although he was in white scrubs with a stethoscope around his neck, he didn't look anywhere near old enough to be a doctor.

He read the chart at the foot of my bed and said, "I'm Dr. Steinberg. How are you feeling, Mr. Armstrong?"

"Pretty good considering."

"Considering you almost got pierced with a knife and lost consciousness when you took a fall?"

"Yes. I'm a lawyer in the middle of a trial. Can I leave the hospital soon?"

"Maybe," he said, shining a light into my eyes. "Do you have a headache?"

"No."

He removed the cuff from my arm. "See if you can stand and walk but go slow and easy."

I was slightly unsteady on my feet until I took a few steps and regained my equilibrium enough to not stagger.

"Do you drink, Mr. Armstrong?"

"Like a fish."

"Lay off alcohol for at least twenty-four hours. You aren't showing any obvious signs of a concussion but if you have head pain or are dizzy tomorrow come back to the emergency room. Several friends are waiting for you in the hallway. You can leave with them after you process out at the front counter."

I thanked him and gingerly stepped through the room's door and into the corridor.

Jarrett, Jim, Ned, and Emily got up from their chairs and came to greet me.

"We're glad you're still among the living," Jarrett said. "Watson told us your attacker tried to stick you with a jagged five-inch blade."

"Was Watson the agent who intervened?"

"Yes," Jim said. "He saw what was happening and drew down on the Mexican. Even fanatics usually surrender when they feel the steel of a gun barrel behind an ear."

Emily silently embraced me and Ned said he was relieved I was okay."

"Thanks for your concerns. Excuse me for a few moments. I need to check out of this establishment."

A woman at the counter presented me with a bill. I handed her my insurance card and she said it would take awhile to obtain approval so I offered to write her a check and have the carrier reimburse me.

She said that would be better for both us and within a few minutes I was in possession of a receipt, the pipe I'd dropped during the attack, and the yellow pad with a hole through the middle.

"Mr. Armstrong, you can leave through the side door the staff uses and avoid the reporters and camera crews at the main entrance."

I followed her advice and Jarrett and Jim helped me through the alternative exit and into a seat in Emily's SUV.

"Is court adjourned for the day?" I asked.

"Yes," Jarrett said. "We'll call our witnesses in tomorrow afternoon's session after Axelrod puts on the FBI crime lab supervisor and the county medical examiner."

Ned said, "Emily and I will bring the witnesses from the reservation with us in the morning. This vehicle is large enough to accommodate all of them."

At our hotel Jarrett and Jim had to assist me again and I assumed the people in the lobby thought I was drunk.

We made it safely to my suite and Jim asked for the car keys. "The Land Rover is still in the courthouse garage and Jarrett and I'll need it tonight. We want to meet Colonel Long at the airport, take him to his hotel, and treat him to dinner. You may not be up to joining us."

"You're right. As soon as you leave I'm crashing and hoping I feel stronger when I wake up."

My plan was temporarily stalled by calls from reporters. I finally pushed the 'Do Not Disturb' button on the room telephone. I also turned off my cell phone but anybody who knew the number could leave me a message.

I slept so deeply I wondered if I'd passed out again but when I woke I did feel slightly better and I was ravenous. The macaroni and cheese with salad I ordered from room service satisfied me and gave me the energy to call the FBI's Tucson office and ask for Agent Watson.

He answered his extension and I said, "David Armstrong calling, Agent Watson. I'm indebted to you for saving my life."

"I'm not sure you're accurately describing what occurred. The Mexican's knife lodged in your writing pad then you tripped and fell. If I hadn't collared him, I expect he would've taken flight instead of continuing the attack."

"I'm still thankful for your quick action. Do you think the Mexican was a Sinaloa Cartel hit man?"

"Hardly. He pulled the stunt with you because he was worried they were after him. He's nothing more than a drug runner like Ruiz was. He told me the men he tried to sell marijuana to in Tucson took his load without paying. Unable to return to Mexico without the money and afraid the cartel would send someone to kill him, he figured getting locked up was the safest thing he could do. His guilty plea to armed assault on federal property will net him a long stretch in prison and be enough time for the cartel bigs to forget about him or be behind bars themselves."

"I appreciate the information and I'm thankful for what you did for me, Agent Watson. I'm sorry you were offended by me having you investigated but surely you know defense attorneys are obligated to perform due diligence on all witnesses against our clients."

"I've gotten over my peeve. My career's been in the toilet lately but today's arrest will get so much play in the media things are looking up for me."

"I hope they are and thanks again."

Next I called Abe, my sister, Mel Berger, Cheryl, Will, Burt, Arthur, and Felicia to alert them to what they would hear and let them know I was all right.

Felicia was happy I wasn't injured and amused by what I said when the nurse asked me who the President was. "I'll be sure to tell Michelle the next time we speak."

"Please do. How's your day going?"

"It was going fine until one of my neighbors came over for tea earlier this afternoon. She's one of the few other blacks I've seen on the island and when I ran into her at the supermarket in Tiburon yesterday I extended the invitation. Her husband owns a chain of soul-food restaurants in LA but they prefer living in Belvedere. The wife seemed like a nice person until she saw the framed pictures of you and me hanging in the house and asked why I was attracted to a white man."

"Reverse racism," I said.

"You betcha. I asked if she'd forgotten love is blind and said when I fell for you I didn't care about your color. You were simply the unique person I wanted for my life partner. I said I'd never met any man of any race quite like you."

"I'm flattered. What was you're neighbor's reaction?"

"She said, 'You're missing out, Girlfriend. No honky can satisfy you like a brother could.' I asked her to leave and I've been upset ever since."

"I've had similar experiences with men wanting to know why I'm attracted to a black woman. Even Abe once asked me if you were hotter in bed than white women I'd been with. I said our sexual compatibility was an exciting dividend of our relationship but not the reason we were together. Why any two people get together is inexplicable and had nothing to do with race in our case. You were just the most desirable woman I ever met and I was going to have you or die trying."

"I didn't make you go that far, though I didn't yield easily, did I?"

"Not at all and the chase was worth the reward."

"If only everyone was as enlightened as us."

"And as good looking, accomplished, and charming."

"The world would be a better place."

We broke into laughter and said goodbye.

I then responded to the messages on my cell phone from friends, fellow trial attorneys, managers of Project offices around the country, and even a couple of former clients.

Jarrett and Jim came to the suite in the evening and found me eating a bowl of vanilla ice cream.

Seeing no other dishes, Jim said, "Is that all you're having for dinner?"

"Yes but I ate a big lunch. How did it go with Colonel Long?"

"Fine," Jim said. "The fare in the little hotel's restaurant was acceptable and he's not a drinker so we left him after the meal."

"He'll be a strong witness, David," Jarrett said. "He holds Ned in high regard. Do you think you'll be okay with going to court tomorrow?"

"Yes, though I'm not feeling anywhere near a hundred percent yet so please cross-examine the FBI lab supervisor and I'll save my energy for the medical examiner. Google the lab's scandals and you'll have all the info you need to thoroughly discredit the supervisor."

"I'm familiar with the routine," Jarrett said and he and Jim left for their own suites after insisting I call if I needed anything.

I went out to the balcony for a pipe smoke. I was craving scotch but I drank only water while I watched the sunset turn the Catalina Mountains pink as I ruminated over the incident that might've cost me my life. The capriciousness of death led me to recall the fate of the Greek dramatist, Aeschylus. A fortune teller predicted he would die from an object crashing on his head so he fled to the wilderness where there were no buildings for anything to fall from. Yet the prediction came true anyway when an eagle mistook Aeschylus's bald head for a rock and dropped a turtle on it to break the turtle's shell, affirming a Greek saying that death often comes on the path we take to avoid it.

CHAPTER NINETEEN

At breakfast on Thursday Jarrett and Jim asked about my condition.

"I'm still a little wobbly."

"Did you watch the news last night or this morning?" Jim asked.

"No."

"Your attempted assassination is a big story and so is the home invasion murder of a popular rancher yesterday afternoon. His property is just outside the eastern edge of the Tohono O'odham reservation and a hired hand living in a cottage on the property saw two Mexican men break into the main house. He was too afraid to do anything himself but he did call 911. When the men were spotted in the rancher's truck on the highway to Tucson a full-scale chase ensued and they were pulled over by State troopers and deputy sheriffs. The officers found several bags of marijuana in the truck along with money and several guns and other articles stolen from the rancher' house where other officers discovered his dead body. His throat was cut the way Ned's parents were."

"Maybe the story will generate some sympathy for Ned. Jarrett, are you ready to cross-examine the FBI lab supervisor?"

"Ultra-ready. He'll be a very fortunate man if something prevents him from taking the stand today because I intend to crush him like a cockroach."

When we got to court Cindy Hill, Axelrod, Metcalf, Charlie, Drew, and even the bailiff said they were glad I wasn't harmed.

And when the session was convened Judge Warren said, "Good to see you, Mr. Armstrong. How are you feeling?"

"Fair to middling, Your Honor. Mr. Hudson will question the FBI lab supervisor and I'll cross-examine the medical examiner. If I tire at the lectern, may I sit?"

"Most assuredly. Do whatever's comfortable. Bailiff, you can bring the jurors in now."

The looks of sympathy I received from the panelists as they came through the rear door and saw my bandaged head were clear evidence they'd disobeyed the judge's instruction to avoid news coverage of the trial.

"Good morning, Ladies and Gentlemen. We'll begin the day by hearing the prosecution's next witness."

Axelrod called Karl Girten to the stand and the man responded to the prosecutor's questions by saying he held a B.S. Degree in Biology from St. Francis University in Joliet, Illinois, and a Masters of Science Degree in Forensics from the University of Illinois in Chicago.

"Where are you employed, Dr. Girten?"

"At the FBI crime laboratory in Quantico, Virginia. During my twenty-two year career with the lab I've worked in every unit of the Scientific Analysis Section—latent fingerprint examination; chemistry; explosives; DNA analysis; firearms and tool marks; hairs and fibers; and materials inspections. I was promoted to Chief of the firearms and tool marks unit in 1996 and in 2005 I was appointed to my present position as Chief of all units of the Scientific Analysis Section."

"Did you personally perform the tests on the evidence submitted to the FBI crime lab in this case, Dr. Girten?"

"No. The various tests were done by primary examiners but I verified the accuracy of each PE's results."

Girten looked at the papers Axelrod showed him, said they were a copy of his report, and Axelrod said, "Your Honor, I submit Dr. Girten's report for identification as Government Exhibit Three and ask for its admission in evidence."

"The clerk will mark the report accordingly."

"Doctor, refer to the exhibit if you need to and tell the jurors the lab's findings."

"I'll begin with the evidence collected at the Johnson family home. Ballistic tests on the twelve nine-millimeter cartridges proved they were fired from a Glock pistol found at the scene. The five nine-millimeter rounds recovered from Sarah Johnson's body were fired from the same pistol. The two thirty-ought-six cartridges found at the scene were fired from the defendant's rifle. The thirty-ought-six bullet recovered from the body of Fabian Ruiz was fired from the defendant's rifle.

"Latent fingerprints lifted from defendant's rifle matched defendant's prints. Latent fingerprints lifted from the Glock pistol matched Fabian Ruiz's prints. Latent prints lifted from surfaces of the Johnson family's house matched

Mr. and Mrs. Johnson, their daughter, Sarah, Fabian Ruiz, and the defendant. Other prints lifted from surfaces in the house were from unknown persons. Prints lifted from the clothing of the three Johnson victims matched their prints and those of Fabian Ruiz. Other prints from the clothing were from unknown persons. Latent prints lifted from one of the two backpacks found at the scene matched Fabian Ruiz's prints. Latent prints lifted from the other backpack were from an unknown person. The latent prints and blood on a knife recovered at the scene could not be matched to any known persons.

"DNA from the blood found in the house was the same DNA as each member of the Johnson family and of Fabian Ruiz. DNA from the semen collected from the vagina and anus of Sarah Johnson was the same DNA as Fabian Ruiz. Hair traces found in the house were from each member of the Johnson family, Fabian Ruiz, the defendant, and unknown persons. Fibers found in the house were from Mr. Johnson's hat, Mrs. Johnson's shawl, Sarah Johnson's skirt, Fabian Ruiz's shirt, defendant's pants, and unknown persons. Impressions in the sand outside the house matched defendant's boots, Fabian Ruiz's shoes, and unknown sources. Tire tracks outside the house matched the tire treads of defendant's truck, and Mr. Johnson's truck and tractor.

"I'll next address the evidence collected at the desert crime scene. Latent prints lifted from Fabian Ruiz's body and from the stakes his hands and feet were tied to match the defendant's prints. Fibers found at the scene were from defendant's clothing. Human hairs found at the scene were from the head of the defendant. Animal hairs found at the scene were from rodents and coyotes. Footprints at the scene were from defendant's boots. And tire tracks at the scene were from the tire treads of defendant's truck."

"Thank you, Doctor. Your witness, Mr. Hudson."

Jarrett approached the lectern and eyed Girten like a panther about to pounce on prey. "You sound very sure of yourself, Doctor."

"My training and expertise and my status with the largest and most respected forensic facility in the world give me confidence."

"Are you infallible?"

"No one is."

"When you used phrases such as 'latent fingerprints matched the defendant's prints' or 'the hair traces were from the defendant's head' were you trying to convince the jurors the findings of the FBI crime lab are irrefutable?"

"Not irrefutable but certainly authoritative."

"Scientists deal in probabilities not certainty. Wouldn't it have been more accurate for you to say 'latent prints were similar to the defendant's prints' or 'hairs were consistent with characteristics of the defendant's hair'?"

"What's the difference? I'm still convinced we matched the defendant's fingerprints and hair."

"Don't you think a cocksure attitude is inappropriate for a person working in the scandal-ridden FBI lab?"

Axelrod said, "The Government objects, Your Honor. If Mr. Hudson is referring to irregularities in the lab brought to light by a whistleblower seven years ago, that's old news and improper impeachment. Dr. Girten was not implicated in those irregularities."

"Your Honor, the defense has a right to counter the witness's assertion that he works for the most respected forensic facility in the world. Moreover, he was indeed implicated by the whistleblower as I'll point out."

"Objection overruled. The witness will answer the question."

Girten said, "I don't consider my attitude cocksure, Mr. Hudson. And I demand to know why you say I was implicated in lab irregularities."

"All in good time, sir. Are you aware of the report the Justice Department's Inspector General issued after the whistleblower accused lab workers of using junk science and giving misleading and often purposefully false testimony in trials due to an ingrained bias in favor of prosecutors?"

"I'm aware those were the whistleblower's allegations?"

"Are you aware the Inspector General confirmed those allegations in over three-thousand cases?"

"He did find fault with some cases."

"Did the Inspector General criticize supervisors for overlooking the faults of workers in those cases?"

"Yes."

"Were you a supervisor in the lab during that time?"

"Yes."

"Was the firearms and tool marks unit you were then in charge of one of the units the whistleblower accused of using junk science?"

"Yes."

"Bullet lead analysis to be specific?"

"Yes."

"Did the Director of the FBI lab admit bullet lead analysis was an inexact science and discontinue the procedure after the Inspector General's report?"

"Yes."

"Is it true several hundred convictions in which bullet lead analysis was introduced as evidence have been overturned so far?"

"Yes."

"Was the lab's lead analysis of the bullets in the assassination of President

Kennedy a major factor in the finding that Lee Harvey Oswald acted alone?"

"Yes, yes, yes, yes, yes!" Girten said in exasperation. "I'll give you as many affirmative answers as you want on the lab's past problems but the jurors must be informed we've made positive corrective changes in our methodology since the IG's report."

"I'll respond to your claim in a moment. First, I want the jurors to hear some of the prominent cases the Inspector General found lab malfeasance in. Is it fair to say the Inspector General called into question the testimony of lab workers in the trials of the Soviet spy Aldrich Ames, Dr. Jeffrey MacDonald, Patty Hearst, Jonbenet Ramsey, O.J. Simpson, the World Trade Center bombers, the Unabomber, Timothy McVeigh, Randy Weaver, and the Branch Davidians?"

"Yes."

"I'll now respond to your claim about the changes your lab has made since the Inspector General's report. Haven't there been continued instances of misconduct by lab workers, including the recent resignation of a technician for the improper testing of hundreds of DNA samples; the indictment for perjury of one of your hair sample analysts; and the discovery of dry-testing by a fingerprint examiner?"

"Those are indications our quality assurance program is successfully rooting out new problems."

"New problems? The improper DNA analysis involves hundreds of old cases and the dry-testing involves thousands. Tell the jurors what dry-testing is?"

"Reporting results when no tests were performed."

"How long did this examiner provide false test results before she was discovered?"

"The QA investigators say the problem goes back to 2006."

"So the problem began under your watch as chief of all units in the lab's crime section and continued until Quality Assurance investigators uncovered the fraud?"

"Yes but not every case the examiner worked on is suspect. In many instances other evidence supported the convictions."

"A dubious claim, Doctor Girten. The FBI crime lab fiascos threaten the integrity of our criminal justice system. Are you familiar with the Innocent Prisoners Project, an organization dedicated to the exoneration of illegally incarcerated prisoners?"

"I've heard of them."

"Defense counsel David Armstrong is the executive director of the Project and he's informed me that of the more than four hundred prisoners the organization has freed so far, more than half of the incorrect guilty verdicts were due to the faulty testimony of crime lab analysts. I now show you the National Academy of Sciences report on forensics in U.S. law enforcement and ask if you've read this report?"

"I have."

"Your Honor, I submit the report for identification and evidence as Defense Exhibit A."

Jarrett waited until Jim provided copies of the report to Axelrod and the court clerk then said, "Doctor, having read the report you must know the Academy found that apart from DNA, not a single forensic discipline in vogue today is statistically reliable enough to be accepted as expert evidence. Do you think there's any possibility the hairs your lab tested didn't come from Lieutenant Johnson?"

"There is some possibility but not much."

"Do you think there's any possibility the bullets your lab tested didn't come from Lieutenant Johnson's rifle?"

"Same answer."

"The National Academy of Science found forensic technicians get hair analysis tests wrong four times out of ten. The ratio of mistakes in ballistic comparisons is even greater. How would you like to be convicted on the testimony of a so-called expert whose opinion was invalid forty to forty-five percent of the time?"

Jarrett let Girten squirm for several tense seconds before saying, "You don't have to answer, sir. The answer is obvious. I'm sorry the complete defense of our client required me to question your competence and integrity but don't you think you have to pay a price for selling your soul to the disgraceful, pro-prosecution FBI crime lab?"

Girten again hesitated to respond and Jarrett turned his back on him and sat down.

Axelrod said, "Dr. Girten, defense counsel was so intent on assaulting your reputation he neglected to give you credit for your good deeds. Were you among the lab supervisors who urged the FBI Director to make major changes in response to the Inspector General's report?"

"I was actually the leader of the group of senior lab employees who met with the Director. He adopted all our recommendations."

"What were those recommendations?"

"To replace the lab director with a civilian scientist; to replace as many agent examiners as possible with civilian scientists; to strengthen the quality assurance program; and to pursue accreditation from the American Society of Crime Lab Directors."

"Have those recommendations been implemented?"

"Yes."

"What percentage of the problem cases identified by the Inspector General have so far necessitated retrials of convicted persons?"

"Around six hundred, less than twenty percent of the total suspected problem cases."

"And as you pointed out to defense counsel, the more recent instances of misconduct by lab employees were discovered by your quality assurance program."

"Exactly."

"I for one laud your long career of public service, Dr. Girten."

"And I for one castigate you for the untold harm you've done, Dr. Girten," said Jarrett. "Did the FBI lab continue to use bullet lead analysis, voiceprint, bite mark, and lip and ear print testing for years after outside scientists debunked those forensic techniques by saying there was no meaningful data whatsoever to support their findings?"

"I suppose."

"Did you personally testify to test results of those techniques during the period in question?"

"Yes. I believed they were valid techniques, especially when considered with other incriminating evidence. I still do."

"So much for us believing you were a lab reformer. When did you stop feeling bumps on people's heads to determine if they possessed criminal traits? Don't bother objecting, Mr. Axelrod. I withdraw the question. Dr. Girten, did only thirteen examiners do the work on the three thousand problem cases identified by the Inspector General?"

"Yes."

"Yet there were and still are two hundred examiners in the lab. If the work of thirteen caused three-thousand cases to be suspect, couldn't the work of two-hundred have caused forty-six thousand suspect cases?"

"You're toying with mathematical possibilities."

"And your testimony toyed with the lives of an unknown number of persons by helping them be sentenced to illegitimate prison terms. Have you ever asked yourself how many people you've deprived of their precious freedom?"

"I've never acted out of enmity for anyone. I've always performed my job as best I could."

"If arrogance, ineptitude, and violation of trust are the best you can do, God help the innocent suspects whose blood, hair, or fingerprints are tested by the bumbling and complacent lab workers you supervise. I suppose we should be comforted by the fact that the FBI Director finally allowed an independent accrediting source to audit your lab's performance. What were the results of the latest audit, Doctor?"

"The Director hasn't released the results of any of the audits."

"And has said he never will?"

"Yes."

"So much for public accountability and so much for you, sir."

Axelrod chose not to ask Girten any more questions and Jarrett faced the jury box. "You two men seated next to each other on the second row paid no attention to the witness's testimony. Yes, I'm talking to you in the red shirt and to the man on your left. You both should resign from the jury. A man's liberty is at stake here."

"Let's have a sidebar, Counsels," Warren said.

We assembled at the bench and he said, "Were you addressing the bus dispatcher and the long-haul truck driver, Mr. Jarrett?"

"Yes, Your Honor. They were talking to each other throughout Dr. Girten's testimony and should be kicked off the panel for their inattentiveness."

"I didn't notice them. Did anyone else besides Mr. Hudson see their misbehavior?"

Ned, Jim, Axelrod, Metcalf, and I all indicated we had and Axelrod said, "They were also cutting up during my direct examination of the witness. The Government supports Mr. Hudson's request for their removal."

"I'll send them home. Is there anything else?"

"Yes," Axelrod said. "Dr. Hanley, our last witness, isn't available to take the stand this morning. He's waiting to be called in another trial that's running behind schedule."

"How long a postponement do you need?"

"I think we should adjourn until Monday to be on the safe side, Your Honor."

"Monday it is. Return to your seats and I'll make the announcement."

Warren pointed to the bus dispatcher and the truck driver and said, "You two jurors are dismissed. The bailiff will see you out."

The men shrugged and departed as asked then the judge instructed the two alternate jurors—the female accountant and the female dentist to take the men's places. "Let this be a lesson to all of you. Paying attention in court is of the utmost importance. The Government's last witness is unable to take the stand today so we're in recess until Monday. Enjoy the extra time off."

CHAPTER TWENTY

I complimented Jarrett on his devastating cross-examination of Dr. Girten and said goodbye to Ned, Emily, Charlie, Drew, and the interns.

As we were leaving court I told Jarrett and Jim I wanted to go to the defense witness room and apologize for the delay to our witnesses. "Especially to Colonel Long. He wasn't planning on being away from home for the weekend."

Jim volunteered for the duty and left us.

Upon his return he said, "Nobody has a problem with waiting until Monday to testify. The colonel told me he's happy for the chance to leisurely explore Tucson on our nickel. The others don't mind the delay either."

We lunched in the Radisson's café and I perked up after having my first alcoholic beverage in twenty-four hours.

The Sauvignon Blanc was a welcome taste and I said, "Shall we take advantage of the gift of time and fly to the Bay Area tomorrow to spend a couple of days with our lovers?"

"Fly as in an airliner?" Jim inquired.

"Yes. I'm not in good enough shape to take us in the Beech jet."

Jarrett said, "A quick trip home would be nice."

Jim agreed and I opened my laptop to access a travel booking site. After a few moments I said, "United has a flight at seven-thirty in the morning that will get us to San Francisco International around ten. They have a return flight at three Sunday afternoon that will get us back to Tucson by five."

"Book 'em, Danno," said Jim, mimicking Jack Lord in the old Hawaii Five-O TV show.

Jarrett liked the schedule too and I reserved us first-class seats on the flights before asking Jarrett if he would arrange for one of his pilots to meet us at SFO and fly us to the Marin County airport in the firm's jet.

"I'll be glad to," he replied. "You look a little pale. Why don't you put your head on a pillow for awhile and Jim and I'll come to your suite at cocktails time."

I did as he suggested but called Felicia and Ned before lying down.

Felicia was excited to hear I was coming to see her. "You're in need of some good loving and home cooking and no one can provide them to you better than me. I'll invite Jarrett, Susan, Jim, Richard, Abe, and Marianne to a dinner party on Saturday to celebrate your survival."

I phoned Ned to say Jarrett, Jim, and I were going away for the weekend and invite Emily and him to stay in the Radisson Sunday night so we could prepare him for his testimony on Monday.

I napped soundly and when I poured scotches for Jarrett, Jim, and me later Jarrett said, "I checked the weather forecast for the Bay Area and temperatures are predicted to be higher than normal Friday and through the weekend."

"How much higher than normal?" asked Jim.

"In the high eighties."

"Still better than Tucson's interminable one-hundred plus degrees," Jim said. "And for a couple of nights we won't be sleeping alone. Let's turn on the local news and see what's being said about today's court session."

We watched a few commercials then the anchorperson spoke to a reporter who was standing on the front steps of the federal courthouse.

Brian, I understand there was excitement today in the trial of the Tohono O'odham policeman accused of the torture-murder of a Mexican drug smuggler.

> Yes, Pete. The cross-examination of an FBI laboratory supervisor by defense co-counsel Jarrett Hudson so thoroughly discredited both the lab and the supervisor the prosecution's case was severely undermined.

> I understand Mr. Hudson also openly criticized two jurors for not paying attention in court and convinced the judge to dismiss them from the panel.

> That's right, Pete. I've been covering State and federal trials in Tucson for several years and I've never seen a lawyer do that before. The lead defense counsel, David Armstrong, is nationally known for his aggressive tactics but Mr. Hudson doesn't have to take a back seat to him or any other lawyer. By

the way, the prosecution asked for a postponement in the proceedings until Monday, ostensibly because their last witness was unavailable to testify this morning. But I'm thinking they needed time to figure out how to salvage their case. Bottom line, big victory for the defense today.

"How does it feel to be in the limelight?" I asked Jarrett.

"I prefer you getting the plaudits and the criticisms so I hope you'll be well enough to take on the medical examiner when we return from the Bay Area."

"I'm sure I will. A little more rest and lots of loving from Felicia and I'll be better than new."

We had second drinks in the suite and wine with our dinner at the rooftop restaurant so I had no difficulty going to sleep despite the afternoon nap earlier.

Friday morning I met Jarrett and Jim in the lobby at six for the drive to the airport. After a quick stop at the priority check-in counter we helped ourselves to a buffet breakfast in United's Red Carpet Lounge.

Our plane boarded on time and as we taxied from the terminal I put earphones on and listened to the pilot talk with a controller in the tower.

My seatmate Jim said, "Do you miss being in the cockpit?"

"You can't imagine how much, Jim. Being in command of your own jet is such an upper I don't understand why more people don't do it. The initial outlay is only in the millions and the ongoing cost of fuel, maintenance, and reserve for new engines is only in the tens of thousands of dollars a year."

"Sounds like a bargain to me. I read somewhere that Oprah's new jet cost fifty million."

"Her plane is a custom made luxury aircraft which is plush beyond imagination, flies just below supersonic speed, and can take her non-stop anywhere on the globe she chooses to go. Your mention of Oprah is *apropos*, though. She was recently quoted as saying owning a private jet was the biggest joy success afforded her."

"And I've always thought driving a Ferrari was a big deal. Oprah probably spends more bucks filling her jet's fuel tanks than my new Ferrari model set me back."

From his seat across the aisle from us Jarrett said, "Ferraris are overrated in my estimation, Jim. My Porsche 911 is all anyone needs in a high-performance car."

"Oh, yeah. Be my guest whenever you want to race. Your German coupe will be sucked up my Italian speedster's tailpipe. And David's English convertible is too big and unwieldy to compete with either of our mean machines."

"My Aston Martin DB 9 Volante is the most beautiful car in the world according to *Road and Track Magazine*," I said then diverted my attention to the sights below.

We passed over Las Vegas, Death Valley, and the Sierra Nevada mountain range before descending to a landing at SFO.

When we entered the cabin earlier I had advised the chief flight attendant of our plans and after the plane pulled into a gate and the door was opened a United ground attendant guided us down to the ramp to a shuttle bus that took us to the general aviation terminal.

Bob and the firm's Eclipse, a very small six passenger jet, were waiting for us there and once we were aboard and he was cleared for a quick, midfield takeoff we made a ten minute flight to Marin County airport across the Bay from San Francisco.

I got out there and Bob took Jarrett and Jim on to Sonoma County airport where the firm's offices were.

Felicia looked radiant standing beside her Mercedes S Class sedan and waving to me.

"Hi, Fellow. Want to go across the road to the He's Not Here Tavern for a picker-upper before we head to Belvedere?"

"As the characters in Robert Parker's novels say, 'we'd be fools not to.'"

Mick, the tavern's owner, and Marcia his girlfriend and waitress welcomed us.

"Two Beefeater martinis as usual," Mick inquired.

"Please," Felicia said.

"Coming right up. No charge for the ice and lemon twists."

"How charitable of you," I said.

Marcia brought our drinks and I asked Felicia if the dinner party was on for Saturday night.

"Yes. I spoke with Richard, Susan, and Marianne and we're all set."

When we returned to her car she gently touched my bandage and said, "Does your head hurt?"

"Only when I'm awake or asleep."

"My poor baby. I'll do my best to distract you from discomfort."

She was wearing a melon-colored, V-cut blouse and a matching mini-skirt. The blouse showed lots of cleavage and the skirt hiked even further up her thighs when she slid into the Mercedes driver's seat.

"Do you like my come hither, sailor outfit, David?"

"Ever so much," I replied, caressing the soft skin of her right thigh as she navigated the car into southbound freeway traffic.

"Don't be diverting my attention from the road. A ticket for texting while driving is one thing. Losing control of a vehicle while being enticed is quite another."

Within a half an hour we were engaging in passionate kissing in Felicia's house on Belvedere Island until I asked if we should indulge in another round of martinis.

"By all means. Bring them up to my bedroom, please. I want to show you something."

What she wanted to show me was her statuesque body lying unadorned on the bed.

I grinned and handed her one of the glasses. "I take it you want to make whoopee?"

"How ever could you tell? Take off everything except your bandage and lay beside me."

I placed my glass on a bedside table and complied with her wishes.

Later, with our martinis in hand again and leaning our backs against the headboard, Felicia said, "Banging your head doesn't seem to have diminished your libido."

"Nothing could, Nisha. You're such a spice in my life you never fail to excite me."

"Keep talking like that and I'll insist you repeat your performance, my dear lover.'

"Never ask for what you aren't ready for," I said, spilling the remains of my martini on her breasts and licking the liquid off, resulting in us not going back downstairs for quite awhile.

We sipped fresh martinis in the kitchen while Felicia prepared lunch for us. Floor to ceiling windows afforded an unhindered view of Angel and Alcatraz Islands, the Golden Gate and the Oakland bridges, and the San Francisco skyline but I was more interested in relishing the sight of her.

She spread pesto sauce on sour-dough bread rolls, added lettuce, tomatoes, and sliced provolone cheese then served the sandwiches at the counter.

We lolled away the rest of the afternoon at the pool swimming and sunbathing.

At twilight we walked down to the private dock and boarded her thirty-foot Pearson sloop. The old but shipshape boat was included in the sale of the property, which Felicia bought at a foreclosure sale. We took *Mischief* out to the Golden Gate Bridge, past the San Francisco waterfront, and back to Belvedere in an hour and half sail.

Supper was a candlelit affair at a small table in the nook between the kitchen and dining room. And the evening was three Scrabble games at the same table prior to our return to Felicia's bed.

CHAPTER TWENTY-ONE

Saturday Felicia and I engaged in outdoor pursuits. We played three sets of tennis on her court in the morning. In the afternoon we hiked to Belvedere Park for a picnic lunch and walked back up the hill to the estate.

Abe, Marianne, Jarrett, Susan, Jim, and Richard showed up at six and Felicia served drinks on the patio.

A prime rib roast was already cooking in the outdoor gas grill and when Marianne, Susan, and Felicia went into the kitchen following the second round of cocktails Abe and Richard took responsibility for tending to the meat.

At eight Marianne, Susan, and Felicia put the roast beef on the table along with scalloped potatoes, asparagus, salad, bread for dipping in the *au jus*, and glasses full of an Alexander Valley *pinot noir*.

Our dinner conversation was dominated by Felicia explaining why Marianne and she were suddenly bubbling with excitement. "You all probably know President Obama and family are leaving for a two week vacation in Hawaii on Monday and stopping over in the Bay Area for twenty-four hours to rest up for the long hop to Oahu. What's been under wraps until earlier today is that Barack, Michelle, and the girls will do their resting here. He accepted my invitation some time ago and while you men were sloshing down booze on the patio I received a call from his chief of staff letting me know I no longer have to keep this part of the itinerary secret. I couldn't even tell you, David."

"Nor could I tell you, Abe," Marianne said.

"I didn't know," Susan said to Jarrett.

"Neither did I," Richard said to Jim.

Felicia raised her glass. "To Marianne. As manager of my Marin County office, she was instrumental in working out the myriad details of the First Family's stay with White House trip planners and the Secret Service. Congratulations, valued associate and friend."

The rest of us also lifted our glasses to Marianne and she said, "Thanks. There's lots of work left. I need to have a cleaning service come in tomorrow and scour this place from top to bottom then stock the kitchen with the specific food and beverages the Air Force One chef insisted on."

"And we should have a florist fill vases with fresh bouquets," Felicia said.

Abe said, "Felicia, you've pulled off quite a political feat considering you resigned from the Democratic Party in disgust three years ago and were reelected as an Independent."

"I'll concede I have a valuable chip to play at an opportune time. But the offer for the family to stay here was genuine. I support the President and like and respect him and Michelle. My only thought was that the setting and privacy of the estate would appeal to them."

"This place would appeal to a maharajah," Richard said.

"It ain't bad," Felicia admitted.

I asked where she would stay while the Obama's were in residence.

"In my apartment above the Marin County office. The schedule is for Marianne and me to be at the Moffett Navy Air Base in the South Bay at one p.m. Monday when Air Force One is due to arrive. The family will have eaten lunch on board so we'll lead their motorcade to the Exploratorium where Marianne has arranged a private tour of the museum for them, which should be a big hit with the girls. We'll then cross the Golden Gate Bridge and come here. Marianne and I will leave as soon as we've shown the family's staff around the house and grounds."

Jim suggested Obama would be so beholden to Felicia he might ask her to be his running mate instead of the vice-president in the election for a second term.

Felicia shook her head. "I doubt that very much, though Barack and Joe are polar opposites in style and personality. When Barack was still in the Senate and listening to one of Biden's seemingly endless and often incoherent speeches he turned to an aide and said, 'Shoot me. Now!'"

Following freshly baked apple tarts for dessert we retired to the patio for coffee and brandy.

As the dinner party was winding down Abe and Marianne impulsively decided to spend the night so Marianne and Felicia could get an early Sunday morning start on their preparations for the big visit. And Abe would drive me to the Sonoma County Airport to *rendezvous* with Jarrett and Jim for Bob to take us to SFO in the Eclipse jet in time to make our United flight back to Tucson.

Sunday morning Felicia and Marianne were so busy getting the house ready for the arrival of the Obamas I called Jarrett and Jim and suggested we return to Tucson on an earlier flight.

They and United were amenable and the rescheduled flight got us to Tucson International a half an hour past noon.

We stopped at Chili and More for lunch on the way to the Radisson. When our waitress brought bowls of steaming hot chili con carne with shredded cheese and chopped onions to the table she studied my face. "Aren't you the attorney defending the Indian for killing a Mexican drug smuggler?"

I allowed I was and she said, "I recognize you from your picture in the paper when another Mexican smuggler tried to stab you. The next Mexicans crossing the border with mayhem on their minds are in for a rude surprise. Ever since the rancher south of here was murdered the owners of neighboring ranches have posted signs in English and Spanish saying they'll shoot to kill anyone they see crossing their property without permission."

The waitress responded to a customer waving for his check and Jarrett said, "There appears to be widespread resentment against Mexican drug runners in the Tucson area."

I said, "One would think so but I fear Tusconians also resent Indians."

Although I was feeling close to normal, I took a nap before our appointment with Ned and Emily.

When they, Jarrett, and Jim came to my suite at five I asked Ned and Emily how their accommodations were.

Ned said, "We couldn't ask for better but the bed is so big I have to commute to Emily's side."

He and Emily smirked in unison and I said, "I'm sure she's worth the trip. Anyway, as we've discussed we want you to rehearse the testimony you'll give in court. Sit in this chair here and I'll stand behind this chair and play my part: Ned, please tell the jurors why you think you were justified in killing the man you're accused of murdering."

Ned related his visit to his family's house, his reactions after he saw his parent's bodies and witnessed two Mexican men raping his sister, and his wounding one of the men and leaving him in the desert tied to stakes.

"Pretty good," I said. "You didn't take long and you spoke with sincerity. I'd like you to sound less apologetic, though. You were within your right to shoot the man who was firing an automatic pistol at you. Try again."

He did three more run-throughs and I said, "Much improved, Ned. Now

Jarrett and Jim will take turns asking you some of the questions we think the prosecutor might pose on cross-examination. This will be a very dangerous time for you in court. He'll try to rattle or upset you into saying things you don't mean to and if he's successful, the probability of the jury acquitting you will be greatly reduced. Go first, Jim."

"How dare you ask us to forgive you for leaving a prisoner in your custody at the mercy of wild animals? You may delude yourself but you can't delude us. We've all seen photographs of the Mexican's devastated body in the desert."

"I wasn't thinking clearly. I ..."

I interrupted. "Way too defensive and don't answer too quickly. Take a moment to reflect first. Jarrett?"

"Mr. Johnson, were you acting in your capacity as a police officer when you shot the Mexican or were you reacting as an aggrieved relative of the three people he killed?"

After a brief hesitation, Ned said, "Both but I don't think the distinction is important."

"Good answer. Jim?"

"Mr. Johnson, do you regret what you did to the wounded Mexican?"

"I honestly don't."

"Why not?"

"I believe my actions were justified."

I told Ned he was getting the idea and Jarrett and Jim continued the mock cross-examinations until I finally said, "We've role-played enough. You're ready for your real performance, Lieutenant Johnson."

Emily said, "That was a downright cruel exercise."

"A downright necessary exercise," Ned said.

"I'm glad you understand," I said. "If you'll all excuse me, I need some time alone to hone the attack I'll launch on the medical examiner's credibility in the morning. If everybody's agreeable to going to the Desert Diamond Casino for another seafood buffet dinner, let's meet in the lobby at seven."

My invitation was accepted and I went out on the balcony to have a scotch and smoke a pipe while I plotted the cross-examination of Dr. Hanley in my head. I'd gone over my notes of the conversation with Dr. Shapiro so many times I no longer needed to refer to them. I felt confident I was armed with enough information to counter the ME's findings.

Among the offerings on the casino's buffet table that night were yellow perch from a county lake and though I took a helping of the native beans I liked so much, most of my plate was filled with the perch, fingerling potatoes, and cole slaw.

The fish was fried to perfection and I twice returned to the table for more before I had my fill.

On our way out of the casino Ned put a dollar in a slot machine and got twenty-five back.

I said I hoped his luck would hold throughout the trial.

Felicia called as I was coming out of the shower in the suite and I said, "How inopportune. You've caught me naked. Unfortunately, we're too far apart to take advantage of the situation."

"Another time, David. How are you feeling?"

"Quite good. I just removed my bandage and if I weren't balding no one would know I was ever less than perfect. How did it go with the First Family?"

"Very well. After Marianne and I got them settled in the Belvedere house we came to my San Rafael office and are having a girl's night out. She's in the kitchen now preparing one of her piquant Sicilian pasta specialties and I'm sipping Beefeaters and talking to the love of my life."

"And I'm talking to the love of my life. When do you get your house back?"

"Tomorrow afternoon. The Obama's are scheduled to take off for Honolulu at three. Call me after court. I'll be anxious to hear how your day went."

I promised to let her know and we said goodnight.

CHAPTER TWENTY-TWO

The line of people waiting for admission to Judge Warren's courtroom on Monday was to the end of the corridor.

Noah Jordon, Jr. was at the head of the line and he greeted Jarrett, Jim, and me. "Good morning, Gentlemen. Emily and I thought it would be good to show support for Ned so I got the word out and commandeered two school buses to bring in fifty-two members of the Tohono O'odham Nation. And Emily had the staff of the Desert Moon Café prepare box lunches for all of us. She says there are only sixty seats for spectators and we were here long before anyone else so the jurors will be looking at a room full of red-skinned faces."

I waved at the smiling Indians. "Thanks for coming. Your presence here is very important. We'll see you inside later."

The officers at the door allowed Jarrett, Jim, and me to pass and we went in to sit at our table.

Not long afterwards Ned, Emily, Charlie, Drew, three Project interns; six guests of the prosecution; and a dozen reporters were admitted.

Our guests took places on the bench behind the defense table; the Government's guests occupied the front bench across the aisle; and the reporters filled the next row on both sides.

When the doors were opened to the public Jordan and the other Indians streamed in to take all but eight of the remaining seats in the gallery.

Ned said, "Tohono O'odhams aren't big spectators. This is the most of us I've seen congregate in one place since last February's rodeo and fair. Leave it to Emily to pull off something like this."

She grinned, the bailiff called the session to order, and Judge Warren came in.

"Good morning, everyone. Are you feeling better, Mr. Armstrong?"

"Much better, Your Honor."

"Excellent. Bailiff, invite the jurors in and Mr. Axelord can put on his last witness."

The panelists came through the back door and took their places in the jury box then Axelrod said, "The Government calls Doctor Roland Hanley."

Hanley came in, took the stand, swore to tell the truth, the whole truth, and nothing but the truth, and Axelrod said, "Good morning, Doctor. What is your employment?"

"I'm a Pima County deputy medical examiner."

"What are your educational credentials?"

"I have a medical degree with a specialty in forensic pathology from the University of Alabama."

"Have you received any awards for your work?"

"I've received several certificates of superior performance from the Medical Examiner and I was the office's employee of the year in 2006."

"Do you have any special qualifications for this case?"

"Yes. In my twelve years as a medical examiner in this county I've performed autopsies on dozens of illegal Mexican immigrants who died trying to cross the desert on the Tohono O'odham reservation."

"Please look at this report and tell me if it is a true and accurate copy of your findings in this case."

"It is."

"Your Honor, I offer Dr. Hanley's report for identification and evidence as Government Exhibit Four."

"Offer accepted."

"Doctor, did your autopsies of Mr. and Mrs. Johnson and their daughter reveal anything unusual the jurors should know about?"

"I found their causes of death to be in accord with the investigating officer's theory of the crime."

"Then let's concentrate on your autopsy of Fabian Ruiz, the Mexican drug smuggler the defendant shot and tortured."

I objected. "The prosecutor's use of the word 'torture' is inflammatory and inaccurate. Lieutenant Johnson is not accused of torturing Mr. Ruiz."

"Objection sustained. Phrase your question another way, Mr. Axelrod."

"Dr. Hanley let's concentrate on your autopsy of Fabian Ruiz, the Mexican drug smuggler the defendant shot and left vulnerable to attack by desert creatures. Did Mr. Ruiz suffer several injuries other than the gunshot wound?"

"Yes. His body sustained multiple traumas."

"Your Honor, may we show the jurors a photograph of Mr. Ruiz's body from the exhibit for the witness to refer to?"

I objected again. "Your Honor, the jurors have already been shocked by one viewing of Mr. Ruiz's body. A repetition might tend to prejudice them against Lieutenant Johnson."
"Overruled."

Axelrod thanked the judge and a picture of Ruiz's cadaver lying on a stainless steel autopsy table appeared on the screen.
"Doctor, you may leave the stand and point out the wounds to the jurors."
Hanley stepped down and put a finger next to various parts of Ruiz's anatomy as he referred to them. "The putatively non-fatal wounds were these molestations of the eyes, fingers, ears, lips, and gums by rodents, insects, and birds. The more serious problems were here—the perforation of the stomach and kidney by a bullet—and here—the burrowing into the chest and thorax and resultant consumption of the lungs and heart by coyotes."
Some of the jurors shuddered at the thought and Axelrod asked Hanley if he was able to determine which wound caused Ruiz's death.
"Not to a medical certainty. More importantly, since this is a criminal case, I did determine the manner of death. Based on my inspection of the scene, the reports of the law enforcement officers involved, and my autopsy, the manner of Mr. Ruiz's death was homicide."
"Could you determine if any of the wounds by wild creatures were caused while Fabian Ruiz was still alive?"
"There were lots of variables to consider and some of them were contradictory but in my professional opinion the traumas to the chest were pre-mortem and could've been a proximate cause of the man's death."
"By pre-mortem you mean before he died?"
"Yes."
"His death must've been indescribably painful."
"Without doubt."
More shuddering and murmuring in the jury box.
"I'll let the defense have a turn with the doctor now, Your Honor."
"Mr. Armstrong?"

"Thank you, Your Honor. Dr. Hanley, I bear no personal animosity toward you and I'll keep this cross-examination as civil as the representation of our client will allow. Your Honor, you allowed the prosecutor to show jurors a photograph of Mr. Ruiz's body. The defense asks permission to show jurors a photograph of Mr. Ruiz's victims from the same exhibit."

"Permission granted."

I motioned to Jim and he projected a photo on the screen of Mr. and Mrs. Johnson and Sarah Johnson lying dead in the living room of their home. The picture wasn't as hideous as the one of Ruiz but the practically severed heads of Mr. and Mrs. Johnson and the despoilment of the pretty and young Sarah was still a ghastly sight.

"Ladies and Gentlemen, this is what Fabian Ruiz did to Lieutenant Johnson's family. This is why Lieutenant Johnson shot him. And this is what provoked Lieutenant Johnson to leave him in the desert. Absent the anguish Ned felt, can we blame him?"

"Counsel is making a speech," Axelrod countered.

"Objection sustained. Rephrase Mr. Armstrong."

"No need, Your Honor. I'll move on. Dr. Hanley, are you aware Dr. Phillip Shapiro will testify for the defense?"

"I am."

"Do you know Dr. Shapiro?"

"Only by reputation."

"What is his reputation?"

"He's a noted forensic pathologist."

"Can you think of anyone whose opinion is more respected than his?"

"Not really. Dr. Henry Lee and Dr. Michael Baden and he are all at the top of our field. Their opinions command equal respect."

"Then I think it only fair to tell you Dr. Shapiro reviewed your autopsy of Mr. Ruiz and will contradict your finding that it was impossible to tell which wounds caused his death."

"What was his finding?"

"He will say the cause of death was the gunshot wound to the abdomen and the mechanism of death was shock from internal bleeding and perforation of the stomach and liver by the bullet. More to the point, he will say you overlooked unmistakable evidence the chest wound occurred after Mr. Ruiz died."

The medical examiner stubbornly said, "I stand by my report."

"We'll see for how long. When you inspected Mr. Ruiz's body did you observe entomological activity in any of his wounds?"

"Maggots were nesting in the wound to the abdomen."

"How about in the chest wound?"

"No."

"Are maggots attracted by blood?"

"Yes."

"Was there blood in the abdomen wound?"

"Yes."

"Was there blood in the chest wound?"

"No."

"How do you explain the absence of blood in the chest wound in light of your contention that it was pre-mortem?"

"I think it's possible one of the first few coyote bites punctured the victim's heart and they licked up the blood their bites precipitated prior to the heart ceasing to pump."

"Did you detect a vital reaction in the chest wound?"

"No."

"Did you detect a vital reaction in the abdomen wound?"

"Yes. The tissue was inflamed and the edges were curled up indicating the body had begun the natural repair process."

"How do you explain the absence of that process in the chest wound?"

"The coyotes got to the heart so quickly the victim's body couldn't react?"

"Oh, Dr. Hanley. You're going so far out on a limb of irrationality you'll never find your way back to respectability. Are you sure coyotes caused the chest wound?"

"Yes. My many autopsies of illegal immigrants' corpses found in the Sonora Desert have taught me a lot about the habits of coyotes and their distinguishing bite marks."

"The tensile strength of a coyote's jaws is not nearly as strong as other predators such as wolves and cougars, is it?"

"No."

"So coyotes are forced to nip and tear at the flesh of prey?"

"Typically."

"Then your quick kill theory is out the window, Doctor. Wouldn't the coyotes that attacked Mr. Ruiz have needed to bite through several layers of skin and muscle to reach the heart?"

Hanley was slow to answer and becoming nervous. I said, "Do you recall your autopsy in the Amber Hester murder case three years ago?"

Made even more uncomfortable by that question, he said, "I do."

"Was Amber Hester beaten with a club and stabbed?"

"Yes."

"Did a defense expert prove you were wrong in finding the knife wounds were the cause of her death?"

"Yes," Hanley said, his voice quavering.

"Did the defense expert prove the knife wounds were caused after her death?"

"Yes."

"Was the man whose fingerprints were found on the knife released?"

"Yes."

"Did the police arrest the suspect whose prints were found on the club and who would've been charged originally if it weren't for your mistaken findings?"

"No. He fled from the country and has never been apprehended."

"Is your habit of making fallacious findings on wounds due to a lack of proficiency or to your intent to bolster the prosecution's position, Doctor?"

"I resent both inferences."

"I'm sure you do but your explanations of your findings in this case show you try to twist facts to support a pre-determined theory instead of doing what anyone with an independent frame of mind—especially a professed scientist—does and develop a theory based on the available facts. You're either a quack or a fraud, sir. How can you expect us to rely on your findings?"

Hanley couldn't look at me or answer the question so I said, "Doctor Girten, I'm obviously causing you stress so if you'll concede your findings in this matter are wrong, I'll stop my examination and save you from even more stressful humiliation and not call Dr. Shapiro when we put on our case."

"My findings may be unconventional but they aren't wrong."

"Do you really think the jury will accept your opinion over one of the most esteemed forensic specialists in the world? I also remind you Government experts are no longer immune from civil liability for negligent testimony."

"I've already said I couldn't tell with scientific certainty whether the abdomen wound or the chest wound caused the victim's death."

"You need to go further or face Dr. Shapiro and a lawsuit. You need to say you overlooked or ignored widely accepted forensic science indicators that the chest wound was post-mortem."

"I don't see the importance but I'll yield the point."

"The importance is there is now proof the victim didn't suffer from the attacks by desert predators. Are you also changing your opinion and saying the Mexican's death was caused by a gunshot wound to his abdomen?"

"Yes."

"Thank you, Dr. Hanley."

Axelrod was on his feet quickly. "Mr. Armstrong browbeat you into those concessions, Doctor. To a scientific certainty or not, are you still willing to stake your professional reputation on your opinion that the victim's chest wound could've been a contributing cause of his death?"

"Defense counsel has put me in a bind, Mr. Axelrod. If he calls Dr. Shapiro to rebut my initial opinion, my professional reputation will be irreparably tarnished."

Axelrod shook his head in disgust and told the judge the Government rested.

Warren pounded his gavel to quell the chatter in the audience and I said, "Your Honor, the defense moves for dismissal of the charge against Lieutenant Johnson. The Government failed to prove every element of their accusation beyond a reasonable doubt."

"Motion denied, Mr. Armstrong. You may put on your first witness."

Jarrett said, "David, if you want to take a breather, I'll handle the colonel and the other character witnesses."

I nodded my gratitude and slumped in my chair.

CHAPTER TWENTY-THREE

"The defense calls Colonel Talton W. Long," Jarrett said.

Long came in. He was wearing a suit instead of a uniform but he still had the mien of the field-grade officer he once was.

He and Ned exchanged salutes and Jarrett said, "Good morning, Colonel. I understand you retired from the 101st Airborne Division as a full-bird colonel?"

"Affirmative."

"Did you command Company C of the 502nd Battalion of the 101st Airborne in the first Gulf War?"

"Affirmative. I was only a captain back then."

"Was Ned Johnson a soldier in your company?"

"He was."

"Did you recommend him for a Distinguished Service Cross and a Purple Heart following a battle with an Iraqi Army unit?"

"Negative. I recommended him for a Medal of Honor and a Purple Heart. He was awarded the Heart but the Division Commander thought a DSC was the more appropriate medal."

"Tell us about the Distinguished Service Cross and Purple Heart medals."

"Except for the Medal of Honor, a Distinguished Service Cross is the highest award in the Army for heroism. A Purple Heart is earned for combat injuries."

"Thank you. Now please tell us about the battle in Iraq."

"The 101st was the first American military unit deployed in Desert Storm. Our Company was dropped deep into enemy territory and we were met with fierce resistance by Iraqi Army machine gunners. We hadn't yet set up our own heavy guns and were relegated to returning fire with M-16 rifles.

The Iraqi's superior firepower caused several casualties before we were able to take cover behind sand dunes. I radioed for armored forces and medical evacuation helicopters but while we waited for their arrival I was astonished to see Private Johnson run onto the battlefield and toss a grenade that took out the closest machine gun nest. He ignored gunfire from the more distant nests and dragged one of his wounded comrades to safety. He repeated this action to save another comrade but was prevented from any further heroics by taking a slug in his right shoulder.

"A .50 caliber machine gun bullet strikes with tremendous force and leaves a big hole so the medic feared Johnson would bleed to death. Fortunately, the tanks and helicopters arrived, the tanks' howitzers destroyed all the enemy machine gun units, and one of the whirly-birds flew Johnson to our main base hospital. In my thirty-year career as an Army officer I never met a braver man than Ned Johnson."

"I thank you for coming all the way from Washington, D.C. to tell us, Colonel. Have a nice flight home."

Axelrod said, "Colonel, are you suggesting the defendant's past display of courage should excuse his recent criminal behavior?"

"Alleged criminal behavior," Jarrett insisted and Judge Warren ordered Axelrod to add the word to his objection.

The colonel fixed the prosecutor with a stare. "Bravery is a character trait and in my experience people of good character only break the law when they have a compelling reason to do so. I also think we should give our war heroes some slack."

"Aren't those questions for the jury to decide?"

"Surely. I just took advantage of the opening you gave me to push the jurors in Johnson's direction. You don't run across many men like him in life and I'll do anything I can to help him no matter how many negative questions you may ask about him."

Axelrod gracefully surrendered. "I'm finished with this witness, Your Honor."

"Mr. Hudson?"

"Me too, Your Honor. We call Emily Crenshaw."

On his way out of court Colonel Long briefly paused at our table to shake Ned's hand, wish him luck, and exchange salutes with him again.

Emily walked from the bench behind our table to the witness stand and Jarrett asked if she was in a relationship with Ned.

"Yes. A very happy one, thank you. We're engaged to be married."

"How did you meet Lieutenant Johnson?"

"I've lived on the Tohono O'odham reservation for eleven years. I'm an advisory member of the Tribal Council and a co-founder of a non-profit organization formed to help the Tohono O'odham people maintain their traditions. Ned was one of our earliest supporters."

"What would you like to tell the jurors?"

Emily turned her head toward the jury box. "That Ned is a wonderful man who has helped many people in many ways on the reservation. I've never seen him express anger towards anyone so the motivation for what he did after his family was murdered must've been more intense than even a friend as close as I am can comprehend. I ask you to judge him fairly. Thank you."

Jarrett released Emily and Axelrod said, "Is your opinion of the defendant biased, Ms. Crenshaw?"

"Naturally. I didn't presume the jurors were so dense the point needed to be made."

Her rapier response caused Axelrod to flinch as if he was cut. He recovered to say, "Giving flip answers to my questions won't change the outcome of this trial, Ms. Crenshaw. I'm done with this witness, Your Honor."

Emily returned to her seat and the Tohono O'odham contingent stood and loudly applauded her.

The judge banged his gavel and patiently said, "You folks may not know you're violating court protocol so I'll give you one warning—don't speak or make any commotion in the gallery or you'll be ejected. Court is in recess for fifteen minutes."

I complimented Emily on her testimony. "You hurt Axelrod more than he cared to let on."

Ned said, "You sure did, Honey. Now I'm not the only man who's learned not to try to match wits with you. Come to the cafeteria with me and I'll buy you a cup of coffee. Anybody else want to come along?"

Jarrett, Jim, Drew, Charlie, and the three interns fell in line behind Ned and Emily but I said I preferred to step outside for a pipe smoke.

"Beware of crazed would-be assassins," Jim warned.

I exited at the rear of the building and went into a park across the street. The pipe tobacco and the walk through the green preserve in downtown Tucson helped me relax from the tension that built-up in my cross-examination of the medical examiner.

When I returned to court a few minutes early I received accolades from Charlie and Drew for my effective impeachment of Dr. Hanley.

The bailiff bellowed for order, the judge returned to the bench, and Jarrett called Wind Runner to the stand.

As old and decrepit as he was, Wind Runner made a striking appearance with his sun-baked copper-colored skin, long white hair, and black suit with string tie.

"How are you today, Wind Runner?"

"I'm fine, my new friend. Would you like me to tell the jurors what I think of Ned Johnson?"

"Please do."

Wind Runner bowed to the jurors, described the foot race Ned once challenged him to and won, and said, "I was impressed he didn't gloat over his victory and I was even more impressed by his bearing. He was only a youngster then but he already exhibited an inner peace from being in tune with nature. I took him under my wing and taught him the ways of our ancestors. Part of his training involved me leading him through the maze of a cave at the base of Baboquivari Peak to the home of our Creator. I can't divulge what one encounters in the maze. All I'll say is I've seen grown men retreat in panic. At the age of fourteen Ned did not. Quite the opposite, he saw the revelation I hoped he would and came out of the cave with the knowledge he needed to be a medicine man himself. We're no longer teacher and pupil. Now we're both practitioners of an art that has healed the bodies and minds of the Tohono O'odham people for six thousand years. The path Ned has walked since then is the measure of his worth to the community and an indicator of the remarkable person Ned is. Don't cage him like an animal for ridding the world of a violent and amoral intruder on our reservation. We honor him for his retaliation against the despicable Mexican man. How could you who don't really know Ned judge him more harshly? Let your hearts guide you to perception and forgiveness instead of misunderstanding and punishment."

There was nothing Axelrod could ask Wind Runner to alter the spell the medicine man cast on the jurors and most everyone else in court so he didn't.

Jarrett helped Wind Runner down from the stand then called Frank Saunders.

The former tribal police chief spoke of Ned's meteoric rise from recruit to the third highest ranking officer in the department in only thirteen years. "And for two of those years he was away fighting in Iraq."

"To what do you attribute his rapid success?"

"Focus, hard work, and inherent leadership skills. Even as a rookie he was head and shoulders above other officers. I've told you and your associates the most amazing thing I ever saw Ned do but I'll repeat the account for the benefit of the jurors."

Saunders went on to describe how Ned pulled a woman and her daughter from a car in flames only seconds before the gas tank exploded. "Other officers and fireman at the scene did nothing to help and if Ned hadn't arrived, the woman and daughter would've been incinerated. I was proud to pin the department's highest award for valor on his shirt. Only two other Tohono O'odham PD officers have ever earned the award and they were both killed in the line of duty."

The testimony of our next witness, Noah Jordon, Jr., was brief and to the point. He only wanted the jury to know Ned and all of his relatives on both sides of the family were among the most respected members of the tribe.

As he left the witness stand I said, "Your Honor, since we no longer need to call Dr. Shapiro our last witness is Ned Johnson."

"We'll hear his testimony after we take an hour's break for the midday meal."

CHAPTER TWENTY-FOUR

I said, "Jarrett, Jim, and I need some time alone with Ned before he testifies so the rest of you have lunch without us. Even you, Emily. I'm sorry but we need him free of distractions."

She accepted my edict without protest and left with Drew and Charlie.

I led Ned, Jarrett, and Jim to the park I was in earlier, saying, "During the break I came across a Chicago-style hot dog stand in here I'd like to try."

They were okay with walk away food too and we were soon chomping on frankfurters in sesame seed buns with mustard, onion, and a fiery homemade hot sauce.

"Maybe my onion breath will keep the prosecutor at bay," Ned said.

"Axelrod's the main reasons I wanted us to talk, Ned. You did well in the testimony rehearsals yesterday but if you're not feeling confident today, I'll ask you a single question and limit Axelrod's scope on cross-examination. He took a real beating in this morning's session and his only chance of salvaging his case is to make you look bad when you're on the stand."

"What's the one question you'd ask me?"

"Do you feel you were justified in killing the Mexican drug smuggler? Your yes answer would be all we'd need to establish an affirmative defense."

"But the jurors will want me to say more so let's go the way we've planned. Don't worry, Tall-Tale Teller. I'm ready for anything the prosecutor throws at me."

Jarrett said, "You're right about the jurors. They'll feel cheated if they don't hear your version of what happened."

"Definitely," Jim said. "And getting to know you is to love you as our parade of witnesses attested."

Ned asked which of our witnesses was the most effective and Jim said,

"In my estimation Colonel Long and Wind Runner were the best. They both had the jurors in the palms of their hands."

We each ate another hot dog then took the long way back to court for the exercise.

Although Ned remained calm, Emily, Charlie, and Drew appeared anxious over his testimony.

The clerk swore him in and I said, "I won't ask you any questions, Ned. Just tell the jurors about the day you learned your family was attacked by two Mexican drug smugglers."

"I was paying them a Sunday visit and when I got to their home I heard a scream for help from inside the dwelling. I took the rifle I keep in my pickup and quietly made my way around to a side window of the living room. I saw my parents lying on the floor with their throats cut so viciously they were practically beheaded. And next I saw my sister ..."

Ned then did what no practice session could've presaged and began sobbing.

I handed him a box of tissues from a table next to the witness chair and asked if he needed a break to compose himself.

He shook his head and wiped his eyes with one of the tissues. "As I was about to say, I next saw my partially undressed fifteen-year old sister being sexually brutalized by two Mexican men. One of them held a knife under her chin while he felt her breasts and the other man was raping her."

Ned's eyes flooded with tears again and he paused long enough to maintain control. "I yelled **AAAAHEEEHAAAAH** at the top of my lungs and fired a rifle shot at the man holding the knife. The shot missed and he ran out the back door. The second man got off my sister to fire an automatic pistol at me. I shot back and my bullet hit him in the stomach. He continued firing the pistol as he dropped to the floor and some of his bullets struck my sister in the chest. I ran inside to hold her in my arms and watch her life ebb away."

Ned interrupted his narration again to take several deep breaths before he went on.

"I bound the wounded man's wrists and ankles and dragged him to my pickup. My first thought was to take him to the hospital in Sells but I was so enveloped in sorrow and anger I left him in the desert and went to tell my police chief what happened."

The courtroom was eerily silent until I said, "I turn Lieutenant Johnson over to the Government for cross-examination, Your Honor."

Axelrod said, "Mr. Johnson, why didn't you call your police department for assistance?"

"My parent's house doesn't have a telephone and there's no cell phone or two-way radio reception in their area of the reservation."

"So you took the law into your own hands and summarily executed a suspect instead of taking him into custody?"

"Shooting a murdering rapist in self-defense doesn't sound like an execution to me."

"Aren't you aware police officers are held to a higher standard than the average citizen when confronting a felony in progress?"

I rose. "The question is misleading, Your Honor. No such standard exists."

"Sustained. Rephrase, Mr. Axelrod."

"I'll withdraw the question and ask another. Mr. Johnson did you ..."

Ned brusquely interrupted. "Mr. Axelrod, my rank is clearly displayed on my uniform and as long as I'm presumed innocent I would appreciate you calling me Lieutenant Johnson."

Thrown slightly off stride, Axelrod said, "All right, Lieutenant. As much as I sympathize with the loss of your loved ones, I'm obligated to prosecute crimes in this jurisdiction regardless of my personal feelings. And the fact is when you tied the Mexican man to stakes in the desert and left him to die an agonizing death you exceeded the reasonable force requirement of a justification defense."

"I don't agree. Mr. Armstrong's questioning of the medical examiner established the man was dead when he was attacked by desert creatures."

"But your intent was for him to suffer from those attacks."

"I'm not sure I harbored any conscious intent. To repeat my testimony, I was reacting blindly to the inconsolable sorrow and anger I was feeling from what the man did to my family."

"Weren't you also feeling the need for vengeance or are you suppressing your true emotions for fear the truth will alienate the jurors?"

"Actually, lying would be easier but I'm not creative enough to make up a better story. Call what I did to the man vengeance if you want. I honestly believe my actions were justified."

"Your chilling lack of remorse is helping me make the case for your conviction, Lieutenant Johnson."

"Nobody's ever criticized me for not regretting I killed the enemy soldiers who were cutting down my buddies with machine gun fire in Iraq. My actions over there weren't considered criminal and my heartfelt feeling is that what I did to the Mexican drug smuggler wasn't criminal either. If I'd exterminated a rabid dog for destroying my family, would you be prosecuting me for animal cruelty?"

Axelrod pondered Ned's question a moment then said, "Twisted logic won't help you out of this predicament, Lieutenant."

I returned to the lectern and asked Ned if there was anything else he wanted to communicate to the jurors before I rested our case.

"Yes. I'd like to comment on the prosecutor's accusation of my lack of remorse. I don't regret killing Ruiz but I do feel sorry for his mother. The land the Tohono O'odham reservation is on was under Mexican rule until the late eighteen hundreds and part of the reservation remains in the Mexican State of Sonora so we've been greatly influenced by the neighboring country. Many of us have Spanish surnames and almost all of us have relatives on the other side we regularly visited until the border was virtually sealed. From this background I understand how much Mexican mothers love their sons and will never abandon them no matter what they've done. Mrs. Ruiz, I have no idea if you're still in this world or gone on to the next but I'll say what I have to say anyway. I'll never forgive your son for his cruelty against my family. If he came back to life tomorrow, I'd kill him again yet my heart goes out to you for the agony of losing him."

Axelrod said, "Do you really expect Mrs. Ruiz and the jurors to believe you care about her?"

"I sure hope they do, Mr. Axelrod. Unlike you, I say what I mean. You said you're only trying to put me in prison because you're paid to, not for any personal reason. I think your prosecution of me is very personal and if I was a juror listening to both of us, I'd believe the one who talked the straightest."

"I'm not on trial here, Lieutenant."

"No but you and I are in a contest to sway the jurors our way and I'm sure the credibility of each of us will be a factor in their verdict."

"We'll soon find out," Axelrod said and returned to his table.

"The defense rests, Your Honor."

"Do counsels need some time to work on your closing arguments?"

"A few minutes to compose my thoughts will do," Axelrod said.

"Me too, Your Honor."

"We'll recess for twenty minutes."

CHAPTER TWENTY-FIVE

I went back to the park for a pipe smoke while I thought about what I would say to the jurors. Over the course of the trial I made mental notes of phrases to use in my summation and as I walked and puffed on my tobacco I came up with a way to take my argument right up to—but not past—the barrier against jury nullification arguments.

"Have you conceived a slam-bang closing?" Jim asked when I returned to the defense table.

"Actually, I discovered a secret weapon I think will steer the jurors to an acquittal."

"The super-duper $19.99 radar gun I saw advertised in *Popular Science*?" Jarrett said, "Or some kind of mind control gadget?"

"I can't say. I can't even tell you, Ned. I don't want to ruin the suspense."

Court resumed and Judge Warren said, "We'll hear from the prosecution first."

"Your Honor, members of the jury, and opposing counsel, we're nearing the end of this trial. All the evidence has been presented and all the witnesses have testified. The only thing remaining is for you to render a decision. I'll begin my attempt to convince you to rule for the Government by commenting on the testimony of Dr. Hanley, the medical examiner who performed the autopsy of the man killed by the defendant. Mr. Armstrong skillfully bullied the doctor into recanting part of his findings regarding the cause of death by purporting a defense expert would contradict those findings. However, in electing to not have the expert come to court and say so in person Mr. Armstrong prevented us from cross-examining his expert, a fact you should consider when you're weighing the medical examiner's testimony.

"As for our other witnesses, Chief Rivas told you when and how he learned of the murders of the defendant's family and of the defendant's reaction to those murders. FBI Special Agent Cuzic detailed the step by step investigation of the Evidence Recovery Team she leads and shared her theory of the crimes. Dr. Girten, the chief of the FBI laboratory's crime section reported the results of the tests his examiners ran on the evidence submitted by Agent Cuzic. Those tests proved the defendant shot Fabian Ruiz and staked him out in the desert to die. One of the defense counsels vigorously tried to impugn the integrity of Doctor Girten and the FBI crime lab but only you can decide whether or not the doctor is credible.

"None of the defense's character witnesses even attempted to contradict the prosecution's evidence, and all Lieutenant Johnson's self-serving testimony left us with is the clear impression he doesn't have a scintilla of contrition for his actions. His appeal for empathy may mitigate his sentence but if you follow the judge's instruction to reach a verdict on nothing but the evidence presented in court, you'll have to find the defendant guilty of second-degree murder. A killing in self-defense is only justified when no more force is used than was reasonably necessary. Shooting Mr. Ruiz in self-defense and to stop a felony in progress was justified. Leaving him in the desert at the mercy of the scalding sun and predatory creatures definitely was not justified regardless of whether Mr. Ruiz died before or after the attacks by the creatures. The severely wounded man was no longer a threat to the defendant or anyone else so leaving him in the desert was done with malice aforethought, an element of the crime of murder. Abide by your duty, distasteful as it may be, and find the defendant guilty, Ladies and Gentlemen. Any other finding would sanction lawlessness by a police officer sworn to uphold the law. The Government seeks nothing more and nothing less than justice. Thank you."

I rose and roamed back and forth in front of the jury box rather than stand behind the lectern. "Madame Foreperson and other members of the jury, before I get into the gist of my summation I'll respond to Mr. Axelrod's comments on why the defense didn't call a witness to contradict the medical examiner's testimony. First of all, nothing the defense does or doesn't do ever relieves the prosecution of their duty to prove their charge beyond a reasonable doubt. And secondly, the medical examiner was so discredited we didn't need to call Doctor Shapiro to add to the medical examiner's misery.

"Now allow me to take us back to last April 30th again. It is a Sunday and Lieutenant Johnson decides to visit his family on his day off. He doesn't yet know they will arrive at their house only a short while before he does. They'd been shopping for a new dress and underclothes for Sarah—Ned's about to be fifteen-year old sister—to wear at her upcoming birthday party. The new underclothes were important since a custom of the Tohono O'odham people is for the father to pull up a fifteen-year old girl's dress and paddle her bottom fifteen times in front of the birthday party's guests. Far from perceiving this as an indignity, the reservation's pubescent girls delight in the rite.

"When Ned gets to the family's house the first sight he sees are the dead bodies of his father—a gentle, caring, former President of the tribal nation—and his mother—a beloved teacher of second-graders for thirty years—lying on the floor with their heads almost severed from their necks. The second sight he sees is one Mexican man holding his sister down and tormenting her breasts while a second Mexican man rapes her. The blood-curdling yell that erupted from Ned—the war cry he repeated for you on the witness stand—was a combination of inconceivable heartbreak and boundless fury, both of which I argue are understandable considering the provocation—and reasonable under the circumstances.

"The Government says they seek justice. So does the defense. Sometimes justice means forgiving a defendant for committing a necessary transgression. Sometimes justice means forgiving a defendant for committing a less grievous misdeed than the one that provoked it. Justice certainly means imagining ourselves in Ned's boots that spring morning and realizing we have no right to judge him. What would we have done if we'd seen our parents lives cruelly shortened and our baby sister's dreams, hopes, plans, her very existence extinguished by a human beast in a whim of unspeakable violence and sexual hunger? Would we have remained dispassionate citizens and simply called 911? Or would we have wanted to kill the human beast ourselves and made him suffer in the process?

"Please don't misinterpret my remarks as anti-Mexican. I co-own a condominium in Puerto Vallarta with the woman I love that we go to frequently. We've found the country and the people much to our liking. Although crime is a problem in some of Mexico's cities, crime is a problem in most of the cities in the U.S. as well, Tucson included. Less than a year ago in another courtroom in this building two white nineteen-year old men from middle-class families here were tried and convicted of a horrible hate crime. They kidnapped three illegal Mexican immigrants and tortured them by pulling out their finger and toe nails, shattering their front teeth with a hammer, burning their skin with cigarettes, and threatening to castrate them before the their screams were overheard by a passerby who called the police. If those Mexican men's relatives had seen what the two boys had done, wouldn't killing the boys have been defensible? Isn't Ned's wrathful killing of one of the cutthroat thugs who butchered his family just as defensible?

"When I was thinking of how I could help you understand why the charge against Ned should be repudiated I remembered what another jury did over three hundred years ago in a trial in England. The defendant was accused of speaking out against the King and the only argument the barrister for the Crown made to the jurors was to return the verdict the King expected. However, the jurors told the judge their consciences wouldn't permit the verdict the King expected. They acquitted the defendant, William Penn, and he settled in America as a free man. The State of Pennsylvania is named after him. In our case the Government expects you to find Lieutenant Ned Johnson guilty. Will your consciences permit the verdict the Government expects? Will you let the massacre of his family go unrequited or will you allow him to leave this courtroom as another free man? Please realize I'm not asking you to nullify the law to do what is right here. The prosecution couldn't and didn't come close to meeting their burden to prove beyond a reasonable doubt that Ned's actions weren't justified and those are the only grounds you need to vote for an acquittal. Follow your consciences and come back with the not guilty verdict this case demands.

"I'll leave you with a story Wind Runner told me about Ned. You heard him tell you one but this is my favorite. During Ned's training to be a medicine man Wind Runner picked up a mole, covered it with both hands, and said, 'What am I holding, my son?' 'A mole, Wise One,' was Ned's reply. Wind Runner asked if the mole was alive or dead, thinking there was no way Ned could answer correctly. If Ned said the mole was dead, Wind Runner would open his hands and let the mole run away. If Ned said the mole was alive, Wind Runner would crush it to death before opening his hands. But Ned didn't choose either of those answers. What Ned said was, 'The mole is in your hands, Wise One.' And so, Ladies and Gentlemen, the case of the United States Government against Ned Johnson is in your hands."

As I turned to walk to my table the Tohono O'odham spectators once again stood and clapped and ignored Warren's demand to stop until he more seriously than previously threatened to have them removed from the courtroom.

They reluctantly settled back in their seats and he said, "If you people interrupt this proceeding again, you'll be locked up for contempt. Mr. Axelrod, you have the last say."

"Jurors, Mr. Armstrong appealed to your emotion. I appeal to your responsibility to the community and to the criminal process and ask you to find the defendant guilty. I trust you will."

Judge Warren said, "We'll recess for fifteen minutes, Ladies and Gentlemen. When we come back I'll issue my final instructions before you retire to deliberate."

CHAPTER TWENTY-SIX

For the first time since I'd known Ned he gave me a hug instead of a fist bump then said, "You're one hell of an attorney, Tall-Tale Teller, but where did the mole story come from? If Wind Runner told you that, he was pulling your chain."

"The story was a fabrication inspired by a technique of the great trial lawyer, Gerry Spence."

Everyone at the table and the bench behind us broke into laughter except for one of the law students who said, "Was making up a story ethical advocacy, Mr. Armstrong?"

"Perhaps not but I wouldn't have hesitated to tell jurors an even bigger whopper if I thought I might help them see the rightfulness of Ned's cause."

Charlie said, "David, I've known you for several years but this is the first time I've seen you work in a trial. The remarkable thing is you really are very good despite all the hype saying you are. The mole story, fable or not, contributed to a masterful summation."

"I've heard there are three kinds of closing arguments. The well-organized one we lawyers outline, the mish-mash of what we actually say in court, and the one we give in the shower later. I just hope the one I give when I'm lathering up tonight isn't the most riveting."

Following more laughter Drew said, "David, you can downplay your performance all you want but I agree with Charlie. Your final remarks were so powerful there was literally nothing Axelrod could've done or said to offset them. You command a courtroom the way a great actor does a stage."

"I'm flattered, though I think the compliments are overblown. A lawyer can only affect the outcome of a trial so much. The facts are the main determinant. Besides, all my trials are a team effort. The assistance and input of Jarrett and Jim are invaluable. What's your read of the jurors, Jarrett?"

"I think the sign painter, the ranch hand, the carpenter, and the Raytheon manager are leaning toward a conviction. I haven't any idea how the foreperson and the other seven jurors will vote."

My intention to ask Jim the same question was forestalled by the resumption of the session.

Judge Warren said, "Welcome back, members of the jury. I'll now give you my final instructions on the law applicable to this case. Copies of these instructions will be left in the deliberation room for you.

"It is your duty to find the facts from all the evidence admitted. To those facts you must apply the law as I give it to you. You must not be influenced by any personal likes or dislikes, prejudices, or sympathy. This means you must decide the case solely on the evidence and according to the law. You took an oath promising to do so at the beginning of the trial.

"Evidence includes the testimony of witnesses and the exhibits presented. Certain things are not evidence. Statements, arguments, questions, and comments by the lawyers are not evidence. Objections are not evidence. Testimony I struck from the record is not evidence. And anything you saw or heard about the case outside the courtroom is not evidence. There are two kinds of evidence—direct and circumstantial. Direct evidence is testimony by a witness about what the witness personally saw, heard, or did. Circumstantial evidence is the presentation of one or more facts from which another fact or facts may be inferred. The law permits you to generally give equal weight to both of those types of evidence but it is for you to decide how much weight to give each of them.

"In weighing evidence, you have to decide which witnesses you believed and which you didn't. You may believe everything a witness said, part of what they said, or none of what they said. To determine the credibility of a witness you should consider their manner while testifying. You should also consider whether the witness was contradicted or impeached, and whether the witness's testimony was reasonable in light of over evidence you believed.

"A cardinal principal of our system of justice is the presumption of innocence of every person accused of a crime unless and until their guilt is proven beyond a reasonable doubt. Presumption of innocence alone may be sufficient to raise a reasonable doubt and require the acquittal of a defendant. A reasonable doubt may also arise from a lack of evidence. Reasonable doubt exists when, after weighing all the evidence, using reason and common sense, jurors cannot say they are convinced of the truth of the charge. Thus, the Government must meet their heavy burden to establish the truth of each element of their charge against the defendant by proof that convinces you and leaves you with no reasonable doubt the defendant is guilty of the charge. If, on the other hand, you think there is reasonable doubt the defendant is guilty of a particular offense, you must give the defendant the benefit of the doubt and find him not guilty.

"The defendant is charged with murder in the second degree in violation of Section 1111 of Title 18 of the United States Code. In order for the defendant to be found guilty of this charge the Government must prove beyond a reasonable doubt the following four elements: First, the defendant unlawfully killed the victim named Fabian Ruiz, a Mexican national; second, the defendant killed the victim with malice aforethought, which means to kill either deliberately and intentionally or recklessly with extreme disregard of life; third, the killing occurred within the territorial jurisdiction of the United States Government; fourth, the defendant's act was not justified under the law.

"The defendant has offered evidence he acted in self-defense. Use of deadly force is justified when a person reasonably believes it was necessary for the defense of oneself or others against the risk of an unlawful and life-threatening attack. A person acting in self-defense must use no more force than was reasonably necessary under the circumstances. Unless the Government convinced you beyond a reasonable doubt that self-defense was unnecessary in this case or that the defendant used unreasonable force in defending himself or others, you must find him not guilty of the murder charge.

"When you retire for deliberation you shall permit your foreperson to preside over the discussions and she will speak for you here in court. Your verdict must be unanimous. Each of you must decide the case for yourselves but you should do so only after considering all the evidence, discussing it fully with other jurors, and listening to their views with an open mind. Do not be afraid to change your opinion if you think you are wrong. But do not come to a decision simply because other jurors think it is right. Do not surrender an honest opinion of the weight and effect of the evidence just to reach a verdict.

"If it becomes necessary during your deliberations to communicate with me, you may send a note through the bailiff signed by the foreperson. I will talk with the lawyers and respond to the note as promptly as possible but you should continue to deliberate while waiting for an answer to any question. In communicating with me in writing or in court remember you are not to say how the jury stands, numerically or otherwise, until after you have reached a unanimous verdict or been discharged. You may now retire and begin your deliberations. If you haven't reached a verdict by five p.m., the bailiff will let you go home. In that event return to court by nine a.m. tomorrow."

CHAPTER TWENTY-SEVEN

The jurors left the courtroom and Judge Warren said, "Counsels, you're free to go wherever you like but be available to return within fifteen minutes until five o'clock. Assuming the jury doesn't come back with a verdict today, the same goes for Tuesday and whatever additional days they may need to reach a decision. We're in recess."

I promised Charlie and Drew I would contact them right after the bailiff called me.

They went out with the interns and I stepped over to the prosecution's table. "Excuse me a moment, Mr. Axelrod and Ms. Metcalf. I just want to say I was impressed by your argument to the jurors, Mr. Axelrod, although I hope the jurors reject your reasoning."

"I won't take it as a personal defeat if they do. I dutifully presented the Government's position but I have some personal doubts as to his legal culpability."

Linda Metcalf said, "My emotions are as mixed as Doug's. We have a responsibility to prosecute wrongdoers. At the same time, we sympathize with Lieutenant Johnson's tragic loss and don't necessarily want to add to his troubles."

"Has Kaya given you any guidance?"

Axelrod shook his head. "Not really. We're all professionals and we know what we have to do. Kaya would've preferred a plea deal but when your client turned our best offer down there was no talk of us not pressing the murder-two charge."

"We'll soon know if Ned will rue his decision. Nice chatting with you both."

I returned to the defense table and Ned said, "Consorting with the enemy, Tall-Tale Teller?"

"I'm not sure they are enemies. They're obligated to argue the Government's case but in this instance they won't be terribly upset if they lose."

"I sensed as much. Axelrod wasn't nearly as tough on me as he could've been and his response to your closing argument was so weak it was like he was throwing in the towel. I wonder if the jurors picked up on his ambivalence."

"Hard to say and I doubt we'll find out today. But you and Emily have to stick around in the remote event the jurors do reach a quick verdict and we do too. I'm going for a pipe smoke in the park. Anybody want to come along?"

They, Jarrett, and Jim did and after we thanked the group from the reservation for coming and got past the reporters, Ned said, "If the judge hadn't thought they were a bunch of ignorant Indians, he might not have let them off so easily for applauding. But they were well aware of what they were doing. They would never act like that in our tribal courts."

We ambled through the park while I smoked a pipeful of tobacco then we sat on benches to nibble on shelled peanuts and savor cones of flavored shaved ice.

Squirrels scrambled for the nuts we tossed on the ground and we listened to the joyous sounds of children cavorting in the playground.

These diversions gave us respite from dwelling on the momentous importance of what was going on in a jury room of the courthouse across the street.

When five o'clock came without the bailiff calling we were as drenched from anxiety as much as we were from the oppressive temperature. So much for Tucson residents claiming the desert location's low humidity made for a bearable dry heat, I thought.

Ned and Emily departed for the reservation and Jarrett, Jim, and I went back to the hotel to swim, sip drinks in lounge chairs, and eventually have popcorn shrimp with jalapeno-ranch dressing served at a poolside table.

We could hear bar patrons angrily reacting to the news on the bar's TV and Jim went in to see what was going on.

When he came back he said, "A deputy sheriff was patrolling the desert adjacent to Interstate 10 north of Tucson when he came upon five suspected Mexican drug smugglers driving ATV's loaded with bales of marijuana. They opened fire on him with AK-47's and left him for dead but he radioed for assistance and was taken to a hospital with non-life threatening bullet wounds. Meanwhile county, state, and federal law enforcement officers in squad cars and helicopters are conducting a one-hundred square mile manhunt for the smugglers."

"Just in time for the evening news," I observed.

"Right," Jarrett said, "And there's no way the jurors can avoid the story.

All their family members, neighbors, and friends will be talking about nothing else."

"And forming into lynch mobs if the mood of the people in the bar is any indication," Jim said.

Back in my air-conditioned suite I engaged in a series of phone conversations.

Cheryl told me things were quiet in the office. "The whole city is quiet, in fact. During the middle of August anybody who can afford to is in the Hamptons."

Will said he liked the slow pace of summer. "The bars and restaurants aren't crowded and there's less competition for the prettiest young women. I'm pulling for you to win the trial and return to the office so I have more time to pursue them."

Burt and Arthur weren't in the Hampton's but they were at their neighboring vacation homes on Yankee Lake in the Catskills.

My sister was glad to hear from me but scoffed when I told her how hot Tucson was. "Have you forgotten your beginnings, my big brother? We can fry eggs on the street this time of year in Arkansas. And do you remember chiggers, the little red bugs that get under your skin and fester?"

"Please, JoAnne. My relationship with Felicia makes me sensitive to racially offensive words. The politically correct term is 'chigroes.'"

"Phooey to you."

Joshua, Mel Berger's live-in servant, informed me Mel already retired to his bedroom.

I said I supposed if I was pushing ninety, I might nod off around eight p.m. myself and Joshua said, "I hear you, Prince David. I was asleep in a chair until you called."

Abe asked me to tell him exactly what I'd said to the jurors and I repeated my closing argument.

He was pleased. "Letting the jurors know something about your client's family and describing what happened to them from his point of view was an effective technique, David. Good writers and speakers know showing is much more powerful than telling. If we read or hear a particular plate of food was delicious, we accept the fact intellectually. But if we read or hear how good the food smelled and tasted, we salivate. When you find out the jury's judgment let me know, please."

"Will do."

I reached Felicia next and asked if the Obamas and their staff left her house in one piece.

"If it weren't for his present and her note, I could hardly tell they were here. The President autographed a copy of his book for me and Michelle penned a hand-written letter telling me how much they enjoyed their stay. She said other than gazing in awe at the views their favorite diversions were the tennis court and the swimming pool. She also invited me and a quote friend to a Labor Day barbeque at the White House. I've been racking my brain to come up with which friend to bring. Do you have any suggestions?"

"What about James, your foreign affairs adviser, the one who was your date at the French Embassy party?"

"He's much too swishy. I considered you, of course, but you're in a trial."

"Which will be over long before Labor Day."

"Then it's settled," she said with a giggle. "Will you come to the White House barbeque with me, Mr. Armstrong?"

"Yes, you mischievous witch."

"How did your day in court go?"

"Good I think. I shattered the credibility of a key Government witness; Ned's character witnesses boosted our case; and Ned's testimony on his own behalf was sincere and moving. Not to mention my summation was brilliant."

"So you expect the jurors to find the lieutenant not guilty?"

"That's not a given by any means. There are several jurors we think are siding with the Government and others may be concealing their intentions. And the white citizens of Tucson tend to be staunch supporters of law and order and biased against members of other races so I'm worried about the verdict."

"Sounds like you're in for a restless evening."

"Very likely. I may have to swill enough booze to pass out."

"Wish I was there to tire you to sleep."

"I wish you had a magic carpet you could fly here to indulge your impulse. But we probably won't have to wait long. In a day or so I should be able to stay with you in Belvedere through the end of the month."

"If we do have so much time together, why don't we go to my chalet in Durango, Colorado instead?"

"I'm all for a cooler clime."

"Me too. There won't be enough snow left for us to ski but we can breathe fresh mountain air, hike on trails with spectacular vistas, go river rafting, fly-fish for trout, and cuddle in front of the fireplace on chilly nights."

We said goodbye and I went onto my balcony and stayed out there drinking scotch and smoking a pipe for some time without calming my anxiety.

Ned called my cell phone at a quarter of eleven. "Am I disturbing you, Tall-Tale Teller?"

"Not at all. I'm as wide awake as you are and presumably for the same reason."

"Yep. When we spoke the night before the trial started we didn't address the real reason we couldn't sleep. Do you know what the reason was?"

"We were scared shitless."

"Bingo. Now we're scared shitless again. I'm scared because the balance of my life is in the hands of twelve strangers and you're scared you didn't do everything you could to be sure those strangers vote for an acquittal. Were you ever in combat?"

"Yes. My reserve Marine battalion was part of the multi-national peacekeeping force sent to Beirut during Lebanon's 1982 civil war. I wasn't in your league, though. I only received a Silver Star. Even though I was shaking so much I could barely hold my rifle, I took out two bad guys and rescued our platoon sergeant."

"All soldiers are frightened out of their wits in a firefight. The only difference is us so-called heroes temporarily overcome our fear in critical circumstances. Wind Runner taught me we can't get rid of the butterflies when we're petrified but we can teach them to fly in formation. Compared to combat, tomorrow should be a cakewalk. At least the jurors won't be shooting back at us."

"Have you entreated your God to give the jurors a little push our way?"

"Elder Brother pays no heed to our individual problems. We can ask for rain or better crops for the Nation as a whole but personal success or failure in this puny existence is entirely dependant on our harmony with nature. How about your religion?"

"I don't have one. If I did, it would be more in tune with yours than anything non-Indians believe in."

"I can see why. When I watch an American basketball player cross himself before shooting a free throw I wonder if the fool really believes a Supreme Being cares whether the ball goes through the hoop or not."

I didn't answer right away and Ned said, "You still awake, Tall-Tale Teller?"

"Oh yeah. I was just wondering if the ballplayer believes he'll go to his version of Hell if he doesn't make the shot."

Ned and I laughed over the ridiculous concept and continued talking until well past midnight when we each said we'd try to sleep.

As I stretched out on the bed I realized why I was especially concerned about Ned's case. Except for an abused wife who killed her husband with a pitchfork when she found him molesting their young daughter in the barn, Ned was the only other client in my career I believed was both criminally and morally blameless.

CHAPTER TWENTY-EIGHT

I was surprised to see Chairman Jordon and the other Indians from the reservation back in court Tuesday morning.

"We'll be here every day until the verdict comes in," he explained. "Our show of support yesterday wasn't meant to be a one-time thing."

"We're glad," I said.

There were only a few other spectators present but all the reporters covering the trial were in attendance, as was Grace Fulton, a CNN legal commentator with her own nightly show. Dubbed Disgrace Fulton by her critics, she was a former prosecutor who began and ended each melodramatic and sensational telecast of her report on a criminal case by yelling, "Guilty! Guilty! Guilty!" Naturally, her show was very popular with television viewers accustomed to such rants by the other irresponsible, over-the-top personalities currently in vogue. From the look I gave her she had to know I was not one of her fans.

At nine a.m. the jurors were brought in and Judge Warren said, "Good morning, Ladies and Gentlemen. Thanks to everyone for being present and on time. You may go to the jury room now and continue your deliberations."

The bailiff led the panelists out and Warren told the rest of us we could come and go but continue to be prepared to return within fifteen minutes.

My suggestion that we go to the park again was met with approval by Ned, Jarrett, Jim, and Emily and in the hallway on our way out we were confronted by Grace Fulton and her camera crew.

"Mr. Armstrong, I understand you won't talk to reporters during a trial. But when a verdict comes in my viewers and I will expect you to give us your reaction."

"Ms. Fulton, all I'll give you is a hard time. You and your show are a disgrace. Now get out of our way or I'll have my savage Indian client scalp you."

Ned repeated the war cry he yelled during his testimony and Fulton and her crew quickly stepped aside amid laughter from the other reporters.

The fleeting amusement was followed by tenseness as we sat on park benches and anxiously waited to learn Ned's fate.

At one point Emily pressed me for a prediction.

I refused to engage in speculation and turned to Jarrett who said, "There are three possibilities, Emily—a verdict of guilty or not guilty or a mistrial. For us to say we have any special insight into what the jurors will do would be grossly misleading. Your guess is as good as ours."

Lunch time came and we bought juices and pre-made sandwiches from a food vendor.

As I was thinking the jurors must be having a difficult time reaching a consensus the bailiff called to let me know they'd reached a verdict.

I used my cell phone to alert Charlie and Drew as we hurried back to the courtroom.

Jordon and the other reservation residents were already there or perhaps they never left but it was more than fifteen minutes before all the reporters and Axelrod and Metcalf returned. As for Charlie and Drew, they breathlessly made it back just as the bailiff called for order.

Judge Warren took the bench and asked the bailiff to bring the jurors in.

Like jurors in every trial I've even been in they didn't look at anyone, kept their eyes down, and gave no signs of their decision.

"Madame Foreperson, I understand you've reached a verdict."

"We have, Your Honor."

"Please hand the bailiff the verdict form."

The grocery store executive did as she was asked and the bailiff gave the form to the judge.

He looked at the form and handed it to his clerk who read it aloud. "We the jury in the matter of the U.S. v. Ned Johnson, case number 209516618, find the defendant guilty of second-degree murder. Signed and dated by Juror Number One, the foreperson."

Ned was stoical but Emily reacted with a sorrowful gasp before the judge said, "Does either counsel want me to poll the jury?"

Axelrod was silent. I said, "The defense does, Your Honor."

Warren looked at the grocery store chain executive seated in the first seat in the box. "Do you concur in the verdict?"

"Yes."

The judge continued receiving affirmative responses to his question until he came to the college student in the tenth seat. "Do you concur in the verdict?"

"Not wholeheartedly," she said.

"Don't say anything more for the moment. I'll poll the rest of the jurors then come back to you."

The last two people in the jury box assured Warren they agreed with the verdict then he faced the college girl again. "You can now explain what you meant by saying you don't wholeheartedly concur with the verdict."

"I held out for an acquittal until some of the other jurors coerced me into voting for a conviction, which they said would send a message to the reservation that we won't accept lawless behavior from Indians any more than we will from Mexican drug smugglers."

"Which jurors were involved in coercing you to change your vote? Don't name them. Just refer to them by their juror number or their occupation."

"The carpenter, the ranch worker, the Raytheon manager, the post office worker, the sign painter, the accountant, and the dentist.

"Madame Foreperson, our college student didn't include you in the group of jurors she says coerced her. Were you pressured to change your vote?"

"I believe the killing of the Mexican smuggler by the defendant was justified but most of the other jurors think he sees himself as being above the law."

"In your estimation were any of the jurors intimidating?"

"The Raytheon manager was the most forceful. He insisted the defendant killed the Mexican drug smuggler out of revenge and told us about an article he read on his computer that reported the torture charge was only dropped on a technicality. I told him you instructed us to not consider anything other than evidence introduced at the trial but he ignored me and he controlled more of the jurors than I did so I finally decided to go along with the majority."

Warren reflected for a moment then said, "Ladies and Gentlemen, I'm releasing you from further service. You may now discuss this case with others, including media representatives, if you wish, and your identities will remain unknown unless you choose to reveal them. Good day."

I waited until the last of the jurors was out of the room before standing. "Your Honor, the defense moves for a mistrial. During *voir dire* several jurors obviously failed to give honest answers when they were asked if they were biased against American Indians. Additionally, the verdict is unreliable because it was obtained by coercion and on information that shouldn't have been considered during deliberations."

Axelrod said, "The Government opposes a mistrial, Your Honor. Even when bias is shown, a new trial is only required if the bias was so prejudicial the defendant didn't receive a fair trial. We don't think that case can be made. And trading opinions in the deliberation room is what jury service is all about."

Jarrett whispered for me to check my email. I immediately did so and scanned the decision he sent me. "Your Honor, the U.S. Supreme Court holding in U.S. v. Cochran is that actual bias of a juror is automatic grounds for a mistrial. Cochran established a two-part test to determine whether juror bias is implied or actual: One—actual bias exists if a juror failed to truthfully answer a material question during *voir dire*, and two—a correct response would've been a basis for a challenge for cause. Both of those requirements were clearly met in this trial.

"The defense also moves for you to exercise your discretion to overturn the jury's verdict and declare a judgment of acquittal pursuant to Federal Criminal Procedure Rule 29."

Axelrod fervently objected and Judge Warren said, "I'll take both motions under submission, review the transcripts, read the case law, and issue my rulings tomorrow morning. Mr. Johnson, you've been found guilty. I remand you to custody. Court is adjourned until Wednesday at nine a.m."

Seeing two marshals hurrying to the table Emily leaned across the railing to embrace Ned. Before the marshals took Ned away they also allowed me to tell him Jarrett, Jim, and I would visit him in the prison right away.

Emily, Charlie, Drew, and we were so stunned we were too subdued to talk. All I could do was silently hold Emily in my arms for a few moments.

Noah Jordon and the rest of the Tohono O'odham contingent left the courtroom without saying anything to us, and the reporters all rushed out to file their reports of the verdict.

As I drove the Land Rover to the federal prison with Jarrett and Jim beside me on the front seat I said, "Although juries are never predictable, the verdict startled me. I'm seriously second-guessing my decision to not have the jurors instructed on voluntary manslaughter."

Jarrett said, "You shouldn't. Ned was in total agreement with the strategy."

Jim said, "And the strategy would've worked if the jurors followed the judge's instructions on the law."

When I parked the car on the street in front of the prison we saw Emily's SUV a few spaces in front of us.

She was slumped over the wheel and bawling. Seeing us, she said, "Ned got into a fight with a U.S. Marshal and they won't let me see him."

"Wait here," I said and we walked over to ring the bell at the counsel's visiting room.

The officer who opened the door was Kelly Collins.

She blushed at the sight of me and said, "I'm sorry you've come out here for nothing, Gentlemen. Ned Johnson assaulted a marshal on the way from court so he's in solitary confinement and not allowed any visitors. I had to turn away his fiancé a few minutes earlier."

"Do you have any idea what prompted the assault, Kelly?" I asked.

"Johnson says the marshal offended him with a racial remark. The marshal denies he did and I'm sure Johnson was a powder keg ready go off after hearing how the jury voted."

"Are you making good grades in all your law school courses, Kelly?"

"I am. Thanks for asking."

"Then you must've learned about *habeas corpus* by now and know attorneys are afforded an ancient right to visit their clients in jail at any hour of the day or night seven days a week. If you don't have the authority to let us see Ned, bring a supervisor in here for me to read the riot act to."

"Excuse me for a moment."

She stepped into an office, closed the door, and came back after a short phone conversation with some one.

"Johnson will be here soon. You can wait for him in the first cubicle over there."

When Ned was escorted in by another officer I noticed a bandage on his forehead and said, "Is the wound from a marshal hitting you?"

"No. One of the pair taking me to their car in the courthouse parking lot said, 'You Indians never learn, Chief. We give you land and let you govern your own affairs but make you pay big time if you break the white man's law. Once a savage, always a savage, I guess.' My hands were cuffed and linked to a chain around my waist so I head-butted him so hard he dropped to his knees. He managed to get back on his feet with the help of his partner but he was so weakened he had no appetite for retaliation. And I assure you his wound is far worse than mine."

Jim said, "A quick, violent attack on a specific part of an opponent's body almost always takes the fight right out of them." He then recounted for Ned the incident with the former Navy Seal.

"How did you know he had toes instead of webbed feet?" Ned asked.

161

"He isn't a fully evolved fish yet."

I said, "Ned, we're devastated by the verdict and you have to be too but tomorrow Judge Warren may declare a mistrial or overrule the jury and declare an acquittal."

"How often do judges exercise those options?"

"Mistrials, fairly often. Reversals of jury verdicts almost never. However, as timid as Warren was at the beginning of the proceedings he did follow the law when we pushed him and the law is on our side in both motions."

"Don't worry about me. Whimpering over life's setbacks isn't in my nature. Tonight I'll meditate, tap into the strength of my forbears, and come to court an undaunted warrior ready for the deciding battle in this conflict."

Jarrett said, "We'll be ready too, Ned. David's taught us to never say Uncle and fight the Government to our last breath."

"Hold on a second," I said and went outside.

Kelly reopened the door when I reappeared with Emily and didn't protest when I led her to the cubicle.

Emily and Ned embraced then I said we should leave since Emily's presence was against the rules.

I told Kelly I wouldn't thank her for allowing us our right to see Ned but I did appreciate her doing so with very little urging.

We walked Emily back to her SUV and took turns hugging and encouraging her to have faith before we got in our vehicle and returned to the hotel.

Later, we ate an early room service meal in my suite then watched a local TV station's six p.m. newscast while we drank scotches.

The trial's verdict was the main story and three of the jurors—the Raytheon manager, the carpenter, and the sign painter—granted interviews to a station reporter in which they stated the purpose of their verdict was to teach Ned a lesson.

The Raytheon manager said, "I'm not sure the Tohono O'odham tribe should have their own police force but as long as they do their officers can't be allowed to commit vengeful acts against suspects whether they're Mexican drug smugglers or not."

The carpenter and the sign painter said pretty much the same thing, though the sign painter added that he thought Ned was a loose cannon and not typical of the reservation's officers in general.

Jarrett and Jim left and I smoked a couple of pipes on my balcony while I tried to think of the best argument I could make to Judge Warren in support of our motions.

Other than Felicia, I cut short the calls from friends and co-workers wanting to commiserate over my defeat by saying I was too engrossed to talk long, which was true.

However, Felicia and I did chat for awhile and, as usual, our conversation left me in better spirits.

Prior to turning in for the night I smoked a final pipe on the balcony, faced myself in the direction of the federal prison, and focused all my thoughts on Ned, hoping he'd receive the silent messages and know I was thinking of him.

CHAPTER TWENTY-NINE

The next morning Jordon and the other Tohono O'odhams were back, as were Emily, Charlie, Drew, and three Project interns. Emily's eyes were red and I imagined she had a sleepless and tearful night. And Kaya Kabotie was at the prosecution table with Axelrod and Metcalf. She and I waved at each other.

Two different marshals than the day before brought Ned to our table. He was wearing a prison jumpsuit instead of his uniform but his dignity was intact and he did indeed reflect the strength he told us the previous night he would show in court.

When Judge Warren came in his face reflected the stress he was under. "Resume your seats. Counsels, I'm ready to rule on the defense's motions but I'll hear arguments from each side first. You first, Mr. Armstrong."

"Good morning, Your Honor. Did you see the interviews some of the jurors gave on TV last night?"

"I did and I took their comments into account in considering the merits of the motions."

"Then all we'll do is remind you the judiciary has the power to check the passions of the community. Although a mistrial would be way to temporarily correct an egregious miscarriage of justice and give us a chance to find more honest jurors for the next trial, we feel a reversal of the verdict is a better solution and, if Your Honor will excuse the colloquialism, a no-brainer. There is no proof Lieutenant Ned Johnson unlawfully killed Fabian Ruiz. Killed him, yes. Killed him in self-defense, yes. Killed him with unnecessary force, no. After the medical examiner revised his opinion and stated under oath the cause of Mr. Ruiz's death was the bullet wound in his stomach and declared he was dead when predators attacked his body in the desert the Government's allegation of excessive force failed, leaving a gaping hole in their case. There was no longer any evidence to support their allegation. Therefore, they failed to prove beyond a reasonable doubt an essential element of the crime and the jury's guilty verdict cannot stand."

"Mr. Axelord?"

"The U.S. Attorney will speak for the Government."

"Your Honor, we support the defense's Rule 29 motion for you to overrule the jury and acquit Lieutenant Johnson ..."

Warren banged his gavel to stifle the rumble of reactions from the gallery and Kaya continued. "When I was in law school and read Berger, the Supreme Court's defining case on due process, the following words stirred my patriotism and my admiration for our system of jurisprudence:

"'United States Attorneys are the representatives not of an ordinary party but of a sovereignty whose obligation is to govern impartially. Therefore, their interest in a criminal prosecution is not that they shall win a case but that justice shall be done. As such, United States Attorneys are in a peculiar and very definite sense servants of the law.' End quote.

"Now eleven years later I can put those words to use. The conviction the Government won in this case is tainted by juror misconduct, defiance of the law, and racial bigotry. We cannot accept a victory obtained against the principles of the Constitution and we implore you to grant the Rule 29 motion."

Warren said, "A judge never sets out to negate a jury's finding and I'm no exception. However, this case is unique. If we were in a mock trial, the moderator could only accept a not guilty verdict based on the evidence presented. As we're in a real world courtroom in a city experiencing almost daily violence, our jury ignored the facts, ignored my instructions on the law, and came back with a conviction, which is why I must set the verdict aside and acquit the defendant. Mr. Johnson, you're free as soon as you're processed out of the detention facility."

Emily laughed and cried at the same time and reached across the railing for Ned as if he were a steady rock in a roiling stream. Jarrett, Jim, and I were close to tears ourselves.

Noah Jordon and the other Tohono O'odhams whooped with joy and swarmed forward to tell Ned how happy they were for him.

The two marshals broke up the celebration and as they hustled Ned out Emily told him she would wait at the prison until he was released.

Before she left I said, "What does everyone think about us partying at the Radisson Hotel where Jarrett, Jim, and I are staying after Ned gets out?"

"I like the idea," Emily said.

So did Noah Jordon, Charlie, and Drew and I said, "We have a lot of celebrants so I'll arrange for a banquet room."

Jim turned on his cell phone and said he would call the hotel.

I gave him a nod of thanks and headed toward the prosecution table. Kaya met me half way so we could speak in relative privacy.

We clutched hands and I said, "I'm thankful for your amazing deed, Kaya. If you get fired, my job offer is still open."

She smiled. "I covered my behind by telling the AG what I planned to do. He didn't try to dissuade me and when I finished giving him the reasons for supporting your motion I think his opinion of me went up a notch or two. He said, 'Well, if fate means for the Indian policeman to go free, your role is to give fate a chance to happen, Ms. Kabotie. We don't want to blemish our record by winning trials that are unfair to defendants.' Now I feel better about accepting my position and I'll reward the AG's faith in me by being tough on people who deserve to be in prison.

"As a start, I'm close to indicting the previously untouchable, long-term, loud-mouth Maricopa County Sheriff for cruel and unusual punishment of prisoners and for his policy of racial profiling undocumented Mexican immigrants. He's been talking about running for Governor. When he hears about my charges against him he'll be running for cover."

"Go get 'em, Kaya. You're one special human being. I'm glad I met you and got to know you a little."

"I feel the same way about you," she said and touched her heart.

On the way out of the courtroom with my exuberant companions Jarrett, Jim, Charlie, Drew, and three student interns a horde of reporters led by Cindy Hill approached.

She said, "You promised us a statement after the trial was over, David."

"So I did. On behalf of Ned Johnson and co-counsels, Mr. Hudson and Mr. Brown, I laud Judge Warren's decision in this case even though he'll be widely criticized in this tough on crime State. He stood tall today and distinguished himself from his peers. Meetings of the Dauntless Federal Judge's Club are very small affairs. I also want to commend U.S. Attorney Kaya Kabotie. Her equally courageous and controversial stand was a game changer. She didn't have to step up to the plate but she did and the law is a beneficiary of her fairness."

"Come on, Armstrong," Grace Fulton demanded. "You're feeding us pap."

"Pap is a good change of diet for you, Dis-Grace. You're addicted to hyperbolic reporting. I've said all I'll say today, representatives of the Fourth Estate. Thank you for your interest."

Jordon must've gotten the word out for not long after my group; Noah; the other Indians from the reservation; and Emily and Ned arrived at the banquet room in the Radisson we were joined by Wind Runner and Chief Rivas.

Rivas gave Ned a vigorous handshake and said, "Don't drink too much, Lieutenant. I expect you back on duty first thing tomorrow morning."

"Yes, sir."

Wind Runner smiled at Ned. "I'm glad you passed another test today, my son. You've given me a reason to drink free Jim Beam firewater."

The large room was set up with a full bar and a bartender. And waiters circulated through the crowd with trays of *hors d'oeuvres* and encouraged everyone to partake of the wide selection of hot and cold food displayed on several serving tables.

I wasn't hungry and I wasn't in the mood for booze so after awhile I excused myself and went outside to call Felicia.

We were finished with our talk when Ned joined me and said, "You having a hard time getting in the spirit of the festivities, Tall-Tale Teller?"

"I suppose I am, Ned. I'm happy we won in the end but I can't help thinking what might've been so I'm humbled and don't want to crow over our triumph. To thumb one's nose at the Gods is hubris squared."

"You're becoming more Indian every day, my friend. I feel the same way and I'll make sure the party stops soon."

After everyone was finished eating Ned, as promised, stood and said, "Thank you all for your support and your well wishes. I can't adequately express how grateful I am to each and every one of you but I hope you'll understand I want to spend some time with no one other than my bride to be, Emily, so we'll say goodbye."

He and Emily departed immediately and many of the other guests followed suit.

Charlie, Drew, Chief Rivas, and Wind Runner were the last to leave and when Jarrett, Jim, and I saw them off too we went up to my suite.

I said, "A close call but we made it across the high wire without falling yet again, Partners. I sometimes wonder when a trial victory will be our last."

"We're too good to stop winning," Jarrett said.

Jim said, "Nobody is, which is why we should continue drinking scotch and enjoying our current success to the fullest."

His prescription cured my melancholy and by seven o'clock I was in my cups and still not hungry so I told him and Jarrett goodnight and said I couldn't fly us to Santa Rosa until the next afternoon because I always abided by the twelve hour bottle to the throttle rule.

CHAPTER THIRTY

Thursday morning I spoke with Cheryl, Burt, Arthur, and Will in my office then with most every one I knew about the trial's result.

Jarrett, Jim, and I ate lunch in the hotel, checked out, and went to the Executive Terminal at Tucson International to turn in the Land Rover.

When I entered the cockpit of the Beech Premier I noticed a feather and a note taped to the control wheel.

The note read:

> This is for you, Tall-Tale Teller. Eagle feathers carry the powerful medicine of the majestic birds they come from. Keep this one with you always to prevent harm as you soar through the sky like other winged creatures. Thanks to you, Jarrett and Jim I've returned to the job I love and if any of you are ever in trouble you can't handle, just call and I'll be by your side faster than anyone would think humanly possible. You gave me my life back and I'll welcome the opportunity to repay any of you in kind.
>
> Your friend for life, Ned.

I showed the note and feather to Jarrett and Jim and radioed the tower I was ready for takeoff.

The message from Ned and the flight to Northern California imbued me with an intense sense of well being.

EPILOGUE

Felicia and I had great fun together in her Colorado chalet and being with President and Michelle for their Labor Day barbeque on the White House's back lawn. Watching them informally interact in a casual setting with their other guests, as well as with the First Daughters, the First Mother-in-Law, and the First pooch was a joy. And I was impressed by how effectively Secret Service agents blended into the background.

Ned and Emily were married by Wind Runner in a native ceremony on the reservation. Emily's parents were there and her younger sister was her bridesmaid. Chief Rivas was Ned's best man. Kaya Kabotie, her husband, and two children; Colonel Long; the agent in charge of the FBI's Tucson office; Dana Parsons, the college student who blew the whistle on her fellow jurors in Ned's trial; Charlie; Drew; Jarrett; Susan; Jim; Richard; Felicia; and I attended as did many other guests, including dozens of Ned's relatives.

The newlyweds honeymooned in a rented bungalow on a white sand beach in Baja California. Prior to returning to the reservation Ned took Emily to the Tohono O'odham communities near the city of Sonora to meet kin he hadn't seen for some time due to Homeland Security's restrictions on border crossings.

Before enrolling at the Embry-Riddle Aeronautical University in Florida Billy Franklin earned commercial, instrument, and multi-engine ratings in the Piper twin I rented for him. The only rating he still needed to achieve his ambition of becoming an airline captain was an Air Transport Pilot certificate.

I divided the rest of the year between managing the Innocent Prisoners

Project and serving the remainder of my one-year term as the titular President of the American Criminal Trial Lawyers Association.

Felicia and I celebrated the Christmas and New Year's holidays in our condominium in Puerto Vallarta, Mexico with Jarrett, Susan, Jim, Richard, Abe, and Marianne.

On my return to work my interest was piqued by the case of Hamid Shirzad, an Iranian-American citizen charged with the attempted detonation of homemade C-4 explosives in the Empire State Building. FBI agents didn't read Shirzad his Miranda rights until days after they began interrogating him and when no other member of the New York Bar came to his aid I volunteered my services.

I unapologetically answered the media outcry over my representation of a terrorist by saying I would gladly represent even Osama bin Laden if necessary because every defendant in an American court—especially those accused of notorious crimes—is entitled to effective assistance of counsel under the Constitution and the Bill of Rights.